CAPTAIN HAZZARD

CURSE of the RED MAGGOT!

AIRSHIP 27 PRODUCTIONS

CAPTAIN HAZZARD: CURSE OF THE RED MAGGOT
An Airship 27 Production
by Ron Fortier and Chester Hawks
Copyright © 2008

www.Airshp27.com
www.Airship27Hangar.com

Cover Copyright © 2008 Mark Maddox
Illustrations Copyright © 2008 Rob Davis
Production and design Rob Davis

ISBN-13: 978-0692412770 (Airship 27)
ISBN-10: 0692412778

Third Edition

1 2 3 4 5 6 7 8 9 0

CURSE
of the RED
MAGGOT!

by Ron Fortier and
Chester Hawks
with Illustrations by Rob Davis

Chapter One
Death on Fifth Avenue

The tall, mahogany-skinned man was breathing quickly, white teeth slightly apart. His obsidian eyes sparkled with a purpose undeniably sinister. A faint spot of crimson glowed darkly in each cheek. Then his teeth clicked together like an inexorable steel trap, and his lips curled like those of a starved wolf scenting his kill.

A block away an advertising clock gave the hour as three minutes of seven. New York's Fifth Avenue was singularly free of pedestrians and motor cars. The bitter cold had sent office workers scurrying homeward from the ice blasts yowling in from the river. Tonight even taxicabs and the lumbering double-decked buses seemed scarce.

The scattering of pedestrians staggered breathlessly against a battering wind. It was too cold for any thought save that of warmth and no one paid the slightest attention to the tall man at the curb.

Up the street a few yards, a smoldering tar vat of the portable type was being attended by an employee of the Department of Streets. The employee adjusted the oil flame under the bubbling mixture and inspected a heat gauge. Apparently the mixture within the vat was not yet ready to pour into the small spot in the street needing repair.

The dark man noticed the repair outfit and a fleeting smile twisted his red lips into a snarling grin. With some difficulty he extracted a white Sumatra cheroot from a silver case and held a windproof lighter flame to its tip. He sucked in the smoke, turned his head slightly. His profile was vulturelike, sharp as if hewn of brown flint. But what he saw made the brief grin return to his red lips.

A man, also in the garb of a city employee, was working over the brass spout of the fire plug between the two stores. The quiet elegance of the store farther from the dark man told of its exclusiveness, that its patronage came only from the wealthy. The sign affixed to its marble front read simply:

VAN DYKE
Pearls

That was all, just those few letters. But behind the sign was an establishment famed wherever fine and costly things were appreciated. Otto Van Dyke dealt only in pearls. His far-flung group of agents purchased pearls from every section of the world, dispatched them to Van Dyke shops in New York, Paris, London and a score of other cities.

And as the dark man shot another glance up and down the street, his dark eyes suddenly became pools of ominous flame, narrowed to glinting slits. He peered sharply at the entrance to the Van Dyke store. Inside, standing near the door, he saw the small, slim figure of a man. The dark man on the curb saw a white handkerchief show as the one within the store wiped at the glass of the door.

From down the block came a faint bong-bong-bong…

It was exactly seven o'clock.

The tall man tossed his cheroot aside on the instant, strode toward the door of the Van Dyke establishment. As his slim fingers found the latch, the last stroke of the hour sounded, and there was a sinister finality to it that again made the dark man's red lips twitch into a fleeting wolfish grin.

Otto Van Dyke, fabulously wealthy owner of the pearl establishment, was short and rotund. He had the apple-rosy cheeks which are part of the German makeup, sea blue eyes of twinkling and ready friendliness, and a trim goatee of white. His hands on the desk were a bit pudgy but they felt tenderly of a bulky something encased in a bag of the softest Carpathian chamois.

"You are about to see the Red Maggot, Herr Floyd," Otto Van

Dyke said with no trace of accent to the man seated across the desk. "It is wondrous, the Red Maggot. A wondrous but terrible thing. For it, kings and princes and just plain people have died. It has devastated whole countries, mein fruend, has the Red Maggot.

"The possessor of the pearl is accursed, for the lust for power seethes in the brain of its owner. It is true, what I tell you. Just as the destroying maggot enters the bodies of all living creatures after death and consumes them, so does the Red Maggot destroy the brain and soul of its possessor. That is why it bears its unholy name. I tell you this because you have asked, because tomorrow you are to leave for the Far East on a scientific expedition."

"But you, sir" Thomas Floyd, famous explorer, said gently, "you are not accursed because of the Red Maggot."

Thomas Floyd was a man of forty-two, rather tall and stocky, deeply tanned of face and with eyes that were half-narrowed as if perpetually squinting against a tropic sun. He was in dinner clothes, wore a small white carnation in his coat lapel. He ran slim fingers through wheat-colored hair slightly tinged with gray at the temples, and smiled at Otto Van Dyke.

The owner of the pearl store shook his head. "For two reasons, Mynheer. One is that I do not trust myself to look upon it save on occasions such as this. The other is that I hold it in trust, as it were, for the safety of that territory we call the South Seas. Should the Red Maggot return to that hell of islands there would be revolts from Manila to Batavia, from Bangkok to the far Fijis. Who knows but what America might also be embroiled in before it was over? I speak truth, Herr Floyd.

"I leave tonight by plane for San Francisco, the first stop on my regular trip to my pearling interests in the Far East. But I dare not carry the Red Maggot with me. The knowledge of its return would spread like an electric spark, cause the superstitious natives to believe the overthrow of the foreign races was at last possible. I would destroy it – utterly – before I would allow its return! But look yourself, Herr Floyd, and feel its malignancy like a blow in the face. The Red Maggot, Mynheer, the only blood-red pearl I have ever seen!"

With those words Otto Van Dyke loosened the draw strings of the chamois bag and placed what it contained before Thomas Floyd's eager eyes.

**"Before him . . . glowed the immense pearl
that was the Red Maggot."**

The explorer gasped. Before him on the desk glowed the immense pearl that was the Red Maggot. Strangely, it was in the shape of a heart, but a living, pulsing heart! It seemed to expand and contract under Floyd's staring eyes, to exude red, incandescent life. Yet it was a malignant life, a red malevolence that had all the horror of eons of unspeakable outrages concentrated in its baleful being. For the Red Maggot had a being, an entity.

Thomas Floyd closed his eyes, drew a sharp breath. The huge blood-red heart beneath his eyes had all at once seemed to intensify its demonical influence in waves of ruby light that battered into the explorer's very soul. He could understand how this accursed thing would gnaw at the brain and reason of men.

Thomas Floyd covered the pearl with a trembling hand. It was soft as velvet to his touch, yet an electrical emanation from it coursed through his veins like liquid fire.

"O-o-over five hundred and fifty grains of-of concentrated evil!" **{1}**

Thomas Floyd faltered. He averted his gaze, narrowed lids, cloaking what was in his eyes.

Through the door of the private office he saw Jubal Beck, Otto Van Dyke's New York Manager; wipe something from the glass of the street door. An elderly clerk was arranging display trays in a showcase. A small clock at Floyd's elbow on the desk softly began chiming the hour, seven o'clock.

"Ja," Van Dyke nodded somberly. "That is why I keep the Red Maggot in a new type of safe that only I, and Rima, my daughter, can open. It is too evil a thing for any man to touch who knows the acid bite of greed, the ambition of unwarranted power. I have not seen it for three years until tonight."

He slipped the chamois covering over the pearl. "Should it return

{1 AUTHOR'S NOTE: The Red Maggot weighted 551.375 grains, which made it possibly the largest pearl in history. Its red color, brilliant as gushing blood, has never been explained, although pink pearls are fairly common. Many jet black pearls also have been found. It must not be thought that a pearl of this size is fantastic. The pearl known as La Peregrina weighted 126 carats-504 grains- and was brought from India to Spain in 1620. It once was owned by Princess Yonasopoff of Old Russia, and at that time was valued at $135,000. The pearl that Cleopatra is said to have melted in vinegar and drunk as a toast to Anthony was valued at $400,000.
A Shah of Persia once owned a pearl valued, in 1632, at over $300,000. But none of them would exceed the value of the Red Maggot with both size and exotic coloring considered.}

to the South Seas it would mean native uprisings, strife, murder –"

Otto Van Dyke broke off short as a black shadow fell athwart the desk. Floyd, whose gaze had been riveted to the chamois bag, looked up. A man stood in the doorway of the office. He was tall, coppery-skinned, had hair as black as India ink. His fulsome red lips were parted in a twisted smile over white teeth. It was the dark man of the sidewalk.

"Herr Otto Van Dyke?" the man asked shortly but there was a hissing quality to the tone remindful of a cobra's warnings. "I am Nomar Samadi, of – of Singapore. I desire a perfectly matched string of pearls as a gift. I want them as quickly as possible…"

The reverberating sound of a dull explosion silenced the man's words. He looked in simulated amazement through the door and to the street. Thomas Floyd was on his feet, brow wrinkled in puzzlement.

In front of the Van Dyke shop, Floyd saw a portable tar vat had exploded, was burning fiercely and spewing up vast clouds of inky smoke. The smoke veiled the large window of the shop. Then Thomas Floyd gasped. Jubal Beck, Van Dyke's manager, had suddenly gone mad with fear. He dashed to the door and threw it wide.

"Fire!" he screamed. "We'll all burn to death! Run – hurry!"

Then an incredible thing happened. The explorer saw it dimly through the murky fog of black that now filled the shop. He recalled seeing a city water department employee working on a frozen hydrant as he had entered. Apparently the explosion had caused it to burst. Water cascaded onto the window and sidewalk like a mountain waterfall.

Floyd's frown deepened. For the water was freezing on the window almost upon contact, completely covering it with an opaque curtain of white ice.

Under cover of the eddying wraiths of black that blanketed the small private office, Nomar Samadi's hand came from the pocket of his overcoat. In his slim fingers was a small glass ball. He surreptitiously dropped it to the rich Turkish rug underfoot and broke it with the heel of his shoe. Instantly an unseen gas permeated the pall of thick smoke. Samadi held a small filter-type mask to his mouth and nose and his snapping eyes peered at the weaving forms of Otto Van Dyke and Thomas Floyd.

The explorer, through the smoke fog, saw a dark blob rush to the open safe, crash the doors closed, twist the combination knob. He was vaguely certain it was Van Dyke. He did not know what had become of the bizarre customer. Thomas Floyd, keen brain racing, knew the burning tar vat and the broken window were not coincidences. They were planned by some master of strategy.

But now his senses reeled as the unknown gas found his nostrils, was gulped into straining lungs. But, he knew, the Red Maggot was safe, locked in the steel vault... A terrible thought struck him. But was the pearl safe?

The gas was taking its toll of Floyd's consciousness. Then, in the murk of the store, he saw Jubal Beck lying across the threshold of the open street door. Ice was caked about him, covered his legs. Smoke continued to pour through the door. At Beck's side lay the old clerk. The man's face was gray. His mouth was open, the tongue protruding.

The fact the clerk was dead wormed its way into Floyd's numbing brain. The attempt at robbery perhaps was an abortive one, but a man was lying dead and that meant murder!

And just at that instant unconsciousness swooped down and Floyd's mind went blank....

Chapter Two
Calling Captain Hazzard

C aptain Kevin Douglas Hazzard sat on the floor in a windowless room, his mind completely at rest. Having spent the first fourteen years of his life blind, he had developed an affinity for the world without light. Here, in his most private chamber, he would sit for hours in solitude, his fantastic intellect active with countless scientific theories and mathematical equations.

Then, when sufficient time had elapsed to exercise his brain, Captain Hazzard, attired only in shorts, would suddenly vault onto his feet and begin a series of physical movements developed to work all the muscles of his amazing physique. A tall, robust figure, in his mid-twenties, Hazzard was the envy of men and the lustful target of the opposite sex.

In the blackness he dropped to the smooth floor and went into his push-up regiments. After doing fifty, he did another set with only his right arm. This was followed by a final fifty with the left. The perspiration beading his magnificent torso was welcome, as Hazzard was only truly happy when he was in motion. Once he'd finished his workout, he exited this unique dark room and made his way through his private quarters. He grabbed a towel from the back of a bedroom chair and wiped his face as he moved towards the windows along the back wall. Captain Hazzard's apartments were located on the top floor of the main building of his private research facility.

The only light in the long, expansive room was a small lamp by his bed and he once again felt comfortable in the semi-darkness. He draped the towel over and around his thick neck and, folding his powerful arms over his chest, gazed out the open window. A cold winter breeze touched his heated skin and for a moment felt good. The glass reflected a weak image of his handsome face beneath his dark brown hair. An almost invisible white scar crossed from his left cheek up over his eyebrow, the one permanent souvenir of his blinding as a child. Blue-gray eyes glimmered with a rare maturity for his years, while a rakishly thin mustache over his upper lip hinted at a soul of mischief, ready to welcome action whenever it came.

Now he stoically surveyed his amazing Long Island headquarters.

Hazzard Laboratories was located on the south-eastern tip of the island and it took in ten full acres. Along the coastline he kept a fleet of ships, to the northwest was his airfield and several hangars which housed futuristic aircrafts of his own design. From his window, Hazzard looked out over small buildings and could make out the long, cigar shape of his fantastic dirigible, Argonaut. Just the sight of it made his longing to getaway resurface in his thoughts. He had been homebound too long since his last adventure.

Hazzard Labs was known world wide as one of the greatest medical and scientific research compounds in the entire world. Employed here were some of the most brilliant doctors and scientists ever assembled under one visionary program. Hazzard Labs, like its founder, existed solely for the progress and betterment of all mankind. It was to the cause of justice that Kevin Douglas Hazzard had dedicated his life and to that end utilized the all the machines and wonders of his famous institution.

After only a few minutes of this rare melancholy, the master of Hazzard Labs headed for the cold waters of a refreshing shower. As the brisk spray rained down on his Herculean physique and cleansed him, a slight mental signal began to sound in his mind. Without batting an eye, Hazzard shut off the water and climbed out of the shower stall and once again took up the large, cotton towel.

This mental itch was nothing new to Captain Hazzard. As a blind child, he had early on developed his remaining five senses to almost superhuman sensitivity. It was at this same time that his remarkable brain began to evolve a special sixth sense, that of mental telepathy. Given the proper circumstances, the lad began to hear others thoughts and likewise send out his own to those with similar gifts.

Later, when he recruited his cadre of agents to help him in his life's mission, Captain Hazzard specifically set out to enlist men who demonstrated strong E.S.P. (extra-sensory-perception) traits. Of his four closest aides, only one did not possess any such abilities; that one being the Montana cowboy and sharpshooter, Jake Cole.

As Hazzard rubbed the towel hard against his biceps, the tickling deep in his thoughts became recognizable as emanating from newspaper reporter William Crawley. Whatever was bothering the savvy newshound was not overly critical as the man was not consciously attempting to make contact. What Hazzard sensed was that his associate was excited about something but still uncertain of its importance. Crawley was also very, very cold.

Although he had been prepared to spend a quiet evening reading the daily lab reports prepared by his Chief of Staff, Professor Washington MacGowen, Crawley's signals caused Hazzard to alter his plans. Going to his closet, he found clean clothes and dressed himself for action. From his military-cut khaki shirt and jodhpur pants to his shiny black cavalry boots, he wore attire that was both comfortable and durable to whatever unexpected conditions he might encounter. His final item of wear was a leather gun belt with an attached holster in which rested a .45 automatic. The belt itself, hooked by a brass buckle shaped like in the form of the letter H, was festooned with half a dozen pouches, each filled with special weapons from his amazing arsenal; all of which the Army boys would have given anything to get their hands on. A true patriot, Kevin Douglas Hazzard always donated his latest weapons designs to the U.S. military, but never until he had personally tested them to assure their efficiency and safety. He would never jeopardize the lives of American servicemen with shoddy materials that often resulted from hasty manufacturing.

Leaving his private quarters, Captain Hazzard touched a button on the wall and a door panel slid open revealing his Spartan office room. He flicked on the lights and sat behind the large desk just as the mental alert flared in his mind. Crawley, calling. Are you there, Captain?

Touching the tip of his forehead with his fingers, the champion of justice replied through the power of sheer thought. Hazzard, here. Go ahead.

This was followed by a series of jumbled images that all tended to merge in a hodgepodge of chaos. Hazzard saw a city street, an explosion, freezing water splashing over a window front. Each image more jumbled than the one more before. He was quick to comprehend what was affecting his associate.

Crawley, your thoughts aren't clear enough. You're too cold. Get out of the cold and find a phone to call me. The images in his head stopped and he took a long breath. Even though he and his men used telepathy on a regular basis, it was always, at best, a tenuous means of communications.

While awaiting Crawley's phone call, Captain Hazzard picked up a strange silver metal band that had been lying on the middle of desk. Beneath the object was a thick folder with MacGowern's familiar scrawl across the top with the words, Mind-Control Apparatus – Results to Date.

Holding the thin, circular band carefully, Hazzard was reminded of how it had been used to turn his cousin, and companion, Dr. Martin Tracey, into a mindless slave. The controller had been beautiful and seductive Circe Yu Sun who had nearly succeeded in creating an army of living zombies.

But Hazzard and his team had foiled her plot and destroyed her secret citadel deep within the Rocky Mountains of Colorado.

Still, Circe had managed to escape in the end and was still out there somewhere. What was she doing? Plotting another scheme to bring about the new world order as envisioned by her maniacal father, Doctor Yu Sun? Or was she scheming a more personal attack on him in retribution for having destroyed her mad dreams?

As much as the woman was evil and his enemy, the human part of Hazzard remembered an all too brief embrace and the taste of sensual, honeyed lips pressed against his own. The contours of her body molding against his as her arms snaked around his neck…

BRINGGGG! RINGG!!

He blinked and put down the silver head band; the image of Circe gone from his thoughts as he scooped up the phone.

"Where are you?" he asked without preamble.

"I'm in a bar off Fifth Avenue," the rough voice of the seasoned reporter answered. "Brrr, it's as cold as a witch's tit out there. Another few minutes and I think I'd have gotten frostbite for sure."

"What did you see, Bill? I sensed an explosion of some kind on the street itself, in front of some kind of jewelry store."

"Not bad, Captain," Crawley confirmed. "But let me fill you in right from the start. Things are still popping down here, even as we speak."

"Proceed," Hazzard said. "And continue to replay the events in your mind. I will see them as your report."

"Alright, Captain. You know who Thomas Floyd is?"

"Yes, the explorer. Although we've never met, we're both members of the Gotham Adventurer's Club."

"Well, I was in a small Italian bistro a few blocks from here about an hour ago, finishing my dinner. I was done for the day and was leaving the place when I saw a cab roll by with Floyd in the rear seat. I recognized him immediately as there was a street lamp on the corner. Floyd is a celebrity and I thought it wouldn't hurt to see where he was heading, so I jogged down to the corner and was in time to see him get out in front of a small shop on the other side of the boulevard."

As William Crawley narrated the events of the past few hours, Captain Hazzard had closed his eyes and allowed his mental cues to enter his mind as he listened to the words. Thus it was like viewing a movie reel in his mind and he could see the details that the reporter had witnessed first hand.

He watched, eyes closed, as Crawley raced along the cold sidewalk and came to a stop across the deserted street from the little shop, now identified as Van Dyke Pearls. Hazzard recalled having visited the establishment once before with his playboy cousin, Dr. Martin Tracey, who wanted to purchase a new bauble for his latest paramour. The staff been very helpful and professional in their knowledge of sea pearls. He continued to listen to the report and receive Crawley's telepathic sending.

Not wanting to barge on in the pearl shop, Crawley decided to wait in the alcove of the Granite Building a few steps behind him. The cold was brutal but at least in the alcove he would be spared the harsh wind whipping over the boulevard. As he stood in the shadows, he stomped his feet and clapped his gloved hands together, hoping that whatever it was Thomas Floyd was doing in the pearl shop, it wouldn't take too long. Or else he'd freeze for sure.

It was only a few minutes later that he spotted the strange dark man who appeared as if out of nowhere and entered the shop, shortly after one of the clerks inside had made a show of wiping the glass over the front door.

Crawley also detailed the city street crew and the foul smelling asphalt repair machine that was making a racket. As a reporter, he was trained to observe his surroundings and even the most mundane detail was worthy of his attention. This included the representative of the Water Department, up the sidewalk from the tar-crew, beating on an iced-over hydrant.

"For a sub-zero night, there was sure a lot of activity going on," Crawley commented editorially amidst his step-by-step report.

"Yes, I agree," Captain Hazzard concurred. "What happened next? After the dark man entered the shop?"

"Well, Captain, that's went everything went to hell in a hand basket. That big, clunky tar making contraption suddenly blew up! Almost knocked me on my butt!"

The tableau unfolding behind Hazzard's closed eyes was horrific as the ruined machine spewed out hot liquid tar like some geyser from the netherworld.

One huge wave slapped against the store window completely covering it instantly. Then red and yellow flames shot out of the broken machine and with them a thick cloud of stygian smoke. As if that weren't enough mayhem, the initial blast had torn off the top of the frozen hydrant and now a huge gusher of cold water was raining over the entire street icing them up quickly.

Steadying himself against the alcove wall, William Crawley had come out onto the sidewalk in the wake of the explosion to see if he could help anyone. When the voluminous black smoke rose up, he had to crane his neck to make out anything it beyond it.

"There was a man lying prone on the threshold of the shop door apparently overcome by the smoke fumes. Then I spotted another man beside the first. This one, an older clerk looked like he was dead, Captain."

"What happened next?"

"Well I heard the wail of a fire alarm and then that tall guy in the dark suit comes stumbling out, half carrying another fellow who looked dazed and hurt. I think it was the owner, Otto Van Dyke, but I can't be sure."

"Understood. Continue."

"Next thing I know, these two no sooner appear than this ambulance comes racing down the street and comes to a stop right in front of them. A couple of the attendants rush out, help get Van Dyke into the back along with the dark fellow and before a crowd can start to gather, they are high tailing back up Broadway. Must have taken them all of five minutes to pick up Van Dyke and that other guy.

"Which is when I started trying to contact you. What with Floyd there, the explosion and that weird character, I thought you might want to look into this."

"You were correct."

"What do you want me to do now?"

"Go to my apartment garage at the Colonial Hotel and get my automobile. Meet me in front of the building in twenty-five minutes."

"You got it, Captain. I'll be there."

Once Crawley had clicked off, Captain Hazzard flicked the button on the intercom box to his left. There were 8 switches on the face, each connecting him to a different part of the complex. This time he was buzzing the main hangar where the majority of his aircrafts were kept.

"Randall, are you there?"

There was a slight pause then a deep voice crackled over the tiny speaker.

"Randall here, Captain." Tyler Randall was his chief pilot and the man in charge of Hazzard's small air force. He was also a veritable giant of man, standing nearly seven feet tall, with corn yellow hair indicative of his Nordic ancestry. He reminded Captain Hazzard of a modern day Viking.

"What shape is the Hornet in?"

"She's good as new, Captain. I took her up only yesterday and the repairs seemed to have given her some extra speed and lift."

The Hornet was a one of a kind auto-gyro that Captain Hazzard and Tyler Randall had designed together. With its stubby wings and huge top propeller, the sleek craft combined the hovering maneuverability of a helicopter with the speed of a single winged airplane. During their last adventure, Circe's henchmen had shot down the fast flying craft with Randall and an F.B.I. Special Agent on board. Fortunately Randall's skill had allowed him to land the damaged Hornet without too much structural damage. Now, after months of repairs and retooling, he was giving her the thumbs up once more.

It was exactly what Captain Hazzard had wanted to hear. "Excellent. Fuel her up and get her ready to fly."

"Roger that, Captain. Where we headed?"

"The City. I want to be there in twenty-minutes."

"Then we'll get you there in fifteen."

Thirteen minutes and forty-five seconds, its engine humming, the Hornet fell out of the night sky over Manhattan and settled with a soft thud on the spacious roof of the Colonial Hotel. Captain Hazzard emerged from the cockpit wearing a brown leather jacket and matching gloves. He gave his ace pilot the thumbs up sign, then in a crouch, raced off as the fantastic little auto-gyro lifted back into the air.

Although Captain Hazzard's base of operations and his actual home were located at his laboratory headquarters in Long Island, there were often occasions that required his stay in New York City. To facilitate such times, he maintained a fully furnished suite on the 32th floor of the Colonial.

A quick elevator descent and the champion of justice was running out the front door past the startled nightshift doorman, Henry. Hazzard gave him a friendly wave, looked down the street and spotted his automobile; a Cord 812 Beverly Sedan, parked only a few yards down along the curb with William Crawley behind the wheel.

Seeing him approach in the sleek speedster's rear view mirror, the newsman began to open the door only to have Hazzard stop him with a wave of his hand. "You go ahead and drive," he called as he got in and took the passenger side leather seat. "And step on it!"

Crawley didn't have to be told twice as he turned on the powerful V-8 Lycoming engine and gunned the heavy sedan into motion. At the same time he hit a dash panel switch and the retractable headlights flipped out, their beams spearing the night before them. Like Hazzard, the reporter appreciated the fine, custom craftsmanship that had gone into the Cord 812 and he loved driving it. Sometimes a little too much, Captain Hazzard thought. Crawley had wrecked three of his newspaper's cars in the last year; one while chasing down crooks for Hazzard. {**2**}

As they careened around a corner, the wheels slid on the icy pavement and Hazzard grabbed hold of the dashboard. "But get us there in one piece!" he added.

William Crawley yanked the wheel around, fish-tailing the Cord back to the center of the lane. He tilted his fedora back on his head and laughed. "Relax, Captain, and enjoy the ride. I know these streets inside out. We'll be there in no time flat."

{**2 AUTHOR'S NOTE:** It happened in Captain Hazzard #1 – Python Men of the Lost City.}

Chapter Three
Green Carnations

By the time Captain Hazzard and Crawley parked in front of the Van Dyke store, the police had arrived and had the situation well in hand. The tar vat had been extinguished and the fire plug was frozen solid. With the still murky shop an oxygen squad worked over the form of Thomas Floyd.

As the pair entered, the explorer moaned, sat up. He was groggy but would fully recover after a few minutes in the fresh air. Inspector Jim Chambers, whom Captain Hazzard knew, was in charge, his brown bowler hat back on his heat as he chomped on a cold cigar. Seated in Van Dyke's private office, swathed in coats and blankets belonging to the oxygen rescue squad, was Jubal Beck. He raised an eyebrow and nodded weakly at the crime-fighter's nod of greeting.

"Are you alright, Mr. Beck?"

"A curious accident, Captain," Beck said huskily. In brief sentences he told what had happened from his perspective. Then he spotted Crawley standing just behind Hazzard. "I suppose you'll be writing it up for your paper and the wire services?"

"Perhaps," William Crawley acknowledged pulling his chewed up notebook and a pencil from his jacket pocket. "It certainly feels like a good story to me. Is anything missing?"

"Missing?" Beck said sharply. Then he laughed. He was a small man, had sandy hair and greenish eyes, an oval face. He had a nervous habit of rubbing at his chin with a forefinger when he talked.

"I'm afraid, Mr.Crawley," he said rather stiffly, "you are trying to be as melodramatic as the police."

He turned and smiled at the scowling Inspector Chambers. "I've told this gentleman time and again there was no attempt at robbery, that nothing is missing. I opened the safe in his presence. Nothing was disturbed. Mr. Floyd was rather emphatic that he saw Mr. Van Dyke lock up a... er... certain pearl during the thick of the smoke."

He shrugged. "It was just a freakish accident and there's no need of making mountains of molehills." Beck snuggled into his blankets.

Captain Hazzard addressed Inspector Chambers. "Inspector, did you locate either of the city men who caused all this smoke and ice?"

"No, Captain," Chambers admitted. "It'll be tomorrow before I can check with the proper officials and find which crews were assigned these jobs. But there's nothing else we can do, sir. Mr. Beck says there was no attempt at robbery, so that lets us out of it. With no crime to investigate, I'm just going to write it up as accident, like Mr. Beck says." He nodded to his men and then shook hands with Hazzard and departed.

"Your clerk is dead, Mr. Beck?" The police might have been finished with things, but not so the champion of justice.

Jubal Beck nodded and pain flashed over his oval face. "Yes. The poor man was in wretched health to begin with. A bad heart, I believe it was. The excitement was too much for him, I suppose." He sighed and shook his head sadly.

"How about this man who barged into Mr. Van Dyke's office at the moment of the explosion? The one dressed in black."

"I can answer that, Captain," Thomas Floyd said, throwing off the blanket over his shoulder and standing. "He was a real odd duck. Said his name was Nomar Samadi."

"Was he a familiar customer?" Hazzard asked Beck.

"I'd never seen him before. He walked into the store with such assurance, I naturally thought he was either expected or was a friend of Mr. Van Dyke. He apparently left during all the excitement. That's all I know."

Hazzard redirected his next question to Floyd. "What were you and Mr. Van Dyke doing when this fellow appeared?"

The grizzled explorer scratched the back of his head for a second trying to recall the events and then light gleamed in his eyes. "I remember. Van Dyke has just taken out the Red Maggot and was showing it to me. Then all of sudden this character was standing in the door demanding service from Van Dyke. He surprised both of us."

"And where is the Red Maggot now?"

"It must be in the safe," Beck offered, looking a bit flustered. "Why, I never gave it a second thought. I dimly saw Mr. Van Dyke rush to the safe with something in his hand, thrust it in and lock the doors. I assume Mr. Floyd saw the same thing. He was closer, in fact, in the same office. That – that damnable pearl is kept in the smaller inner safe."

Beck's shoulders moved in evident disgust. "I never touched the accursed thing. Only Mr. Van Dyke and Miss Rima have the combination. She's at Eastgate College, you know, fifty miles from here, taking a post-graduate course in chemistry."

"Ah, yes, Miss Rima. I've met the young lady."

Kevin Douglas Hazzard often attended charity functions throughout the city. A man of power and wealth, he was on the invitation lists of all the social and political bigwigs of the city. He had encountered the lovely Rima Van Dyke at several fundraisers hosted by mutual acquaintances. She had seemed to him a very intelligent, competent young lady.

"What of Mr. Van Dyke? Have you heard anything from him?" Hazzard inquired. "Mr.Crawley informs me, with the aid of this Mr. Samadi, he was taken in an ambulance to a nearby hospital."

"It looked like he had swallowed a great deal of smoke and was having trouble breathing," Beck explained. "It is strange that he hasn't called. Mr. Van Dyke is normally very thoughtful..." At that second the telephone on the desk started ringing. Beck picked it up and put the receiver to his ear.

He listened for a few minutes, then said, "Very well, thank you for calling and relaying the message. Good-bye." He hung up and look at the others, smiling. "That was the ticket office at the New York airport. Mr. Van Dyke just left for the West; he asked the ticket man to phone me and say he is well and not to worry."

"Doesn't this seem a bit rushed?" Hazzard frowned. "Wouldn't he want to make sure everything here was back to normal before leaving like that?"

"My dear Captain," Beck was clearly put-out now by the continued questioning. "Mr. Van Dyke had planned this trip for weeks. If he didn't make that particular flight out, he would miss his connecting ship in San Francisco.

"It's apparent he recovered fully in the ambulance, caught a cab to his downtown apartment to pick up his ticket and then proceeded to airport. I know for a fact, he had had his bags sent there earlier in the day."

Captain Hazzard folded his arms across his chest and moved away from the agitated Beck, leaving it to William Crawley to take up the slack. "Still, you have to admit it sounds more than strange. The store is nearly destroyed by some bizarre accident and then the owner packs up and flies off for the West coast." As he talked, the newshound was scribbling in his notebook.

Beck shrugged once more. "Think what you will, there is is absolutely nothing to be made of this but what it is, an accident!" His thin face sobered and the forefinger rubbed at his chin. "By the way, if you don't mind, how is you got here so quickly, Crawley?"

The reporter looked at Beck and Thomas Floyd and a sheepish grin spread over his long face. "Well, to tell you the truth, I spotted Mr. Floyd coming here and decided to follow him."

"You followed me?" the explorer tilted his head looking perplexed. "But why?"

"Come on, Mr. Floyd, you're a world famous traveler and explorer," Crawley replied. "A celebrity. Seeing you going into a fancy jewelry shop just got my nose itching. So I camped out across the street in the front entrance of the Granite Building hoping to maybe catch some kind of story and, brother, did I ever."

"So you saw the explosion and everything?" Floyd deduced.

"You bet. And when I saw Mr. Van Dyke being hauled away in that ambulance by the dark man, I called Captain Hazzard and here we are."

"Don't be so proud of yourself," Beck laughed. "As you can clearly see, there is no story here for you."

Crawley was going to say something else when Captain Hazzard laid a hand on his shoulder and said, "I agree, Mr. Beck. We won't bother you any further." At the exact time, Hazzard was sending the reporter a mental message; Bill, there is something on the floor just beneath the desk. Crawley stiffened slightly, but did not let on that anything unusual was going on.

I need you to drop your pencil beside it so that you can pick up whatever it is without Beck seeing you do it.

"No bother at all," Beck rose and shook Hazzard's hand, obviously relieved to be rid of them. "I appreciate your concern, Captain."

Crawley started to cram his notebook and pencil back into his pocket when the pencil flipped out of his fingers. He grinned at Beck and Floyd and turned, dropped to one knee and fished on the floor for it. With his back to them, they could not see him also retrieve the object Hazzard had spotted.

Captain Hazzard turned to Thomas Floyd. "I've my car outside, Mr. Floyd. I'll be glad to run you to your apartment."

"That would be great, thanks." The explorer shook hands with Jubal Beck and then he, Captain Hazzard and William Crawley exited pearl shop. Together they walked over the slippery sidewalk to where the Cord 812 was parked. At the sight of it, Floyd whistled. "You travel in style, Captain."

Crawley climbed into the back, allowing Floyd to take the front passenger seat with Hazzard getting in behind the wheel. A moment later he shifted gears and took the corner of Fifty-first street at high speed.

Thomas Floyd showed his surprise. "Rather in a hurry, eh, Captain? Getting me home is no case of life or death..."

"To you, no" Hazzard snapped. "But I think Rima Van Dyke is in deadly danger!"

"Nonsense," the explorer chuckled. "You're like the police, Hazzard. Trying to make something sensational out of a simple accident. I'd heard better things of you, sir. That you were a clear thinking, steady sort and not one to go off half-cocked like this."

Captain Hazzard smiled grimly. He had taken an instant liking to Floyd. "You forget you were overcome by a gas, were you not?"

Thomas Floyd laughed. "Why, that was nothing but the effects of the tar smoke. That's all. Sure, I'll admit it overcame me pretty easily. But a lethal gas!" He shook his head, a rather patronizing smile curving his lips.

"Mr. Floyd, since when have you gone in for green carnations?" Captain Hazzard asked nonchalantly.

"Green carnations! What..." The explorer threw back his collar of his overcoat, took the flower from his lapel and held it so the dash light shone on it. The carnation was deep emerald green!

"The reason you went under so easily, Mr. Floyd," Hazzard stated, "was because there was a discharge of etherolate gas in that office. I know, because that particular gas will turn the petals of a white flower a deep green. It has an anesthetizing effect on humans, acts exactly as does ether. And here's another premise you'll appreciate."

Without taking his eyes off the road, Captain Hazzard put his right hand up and back. "Bill."

"Got it right here." Crawley pulled something out of his jacket and placed it in Hazzard's hand.

"What is that thing?" Floyd squinted to scrutinize the thing closer. Then his eyes widened as he realized he was looking at; a filter-type gas mask.

"I see you recognize it for what it is," Hazzard said, handing it to the startled adventurer. "Crawley picked it up from under the desk when he dropped his pencil. I didn't want Beck to see what we'd found."

Thomas Floyd continued to study the mask, turning it around in his hands. "But this...implies.."

"It implies, Mr. Floyd, that you don't find etherolate gas and filter masks in a room unless something nefarious is under way. Can we agree on that?"

"Most definitely!" Thomas Floyd exclaimed, running a hand through his wheat-colored hair. "But why this mad rush to East-gate College? Miss Van Dyke is undoubtedly safe in her dormitory. I can't see how she would be affected by this?"

"Let's hope she is safe. The Red Maggot apparently is within the special vault, or Van Dyke would not have left on his trip. But I feel there's something queer to the whole affair. Beck firmly believes nothing is missing. He may be right.

"But if Van Dyke and Rima are the only ones who know the combination of the inner safe, and the robbery was a failure, it remains that her safety is endangered, for the ones trying for the Red Maggot may force the girl too open the safe. I honestly believe Beck is unaware it was a planned attempt. For the time being we won't let him know it was an attempt."

Captain Hazzard threw his speedy Cord 812 around another corner, straightened out on the main road which led to the little town of Newcastle, where Eastgate College was located. A feeling of danger, of menace, impinged on his subconscious. There was something deadly, malignant in the perfectly planned affair on Fifth Avenue which, in its perfection, implied menace yet to come. And that led, without doubt, to Rima Van Dyke.

"Floyd," Crawley leaned forward from the back seat. "Did you get a real good look at that dark man who appeared in the office? I was too far away, when he came down the street, to get a close look at his mug."

"Not a good one," Thomas Floyd confessed. "Things happened pretty fast after that tar machine blew up. When he showed up, I just thought he was some kind of special customer. I got to my feet and stood back. Mr. Van Dyke apparently covered the Red Maggot." As best he could, the explorer tried to describe the man who had identified himself as Nomar Samadi.

"A sinister name," Captain Hazzard remarked. "In medieval times, Samadi meant an orgy celebrated by demons and sorcerers. Please, go on."

"Well, the smoke and water started. Beck went mad with fright. Anyone who lost his head so completely couldn't have had anything to do with planning the robbery, so that lets him out in my book. The smoke was so dense I couldn't see anything. That's all I know, gentlemen."

William Crawley finished a sentence in his notepad. "Otto Van Dyke is a very wealthy man. Crooks have tried to get him in the past, particularly for that cursed Red Maggot. I've known the old German for years, and he's told me of the attempts. It once was owned by some Khmer King. He lost his country because of the madness it instilled in his brain, they say. Van Dyke has been safe from this madness because he is stolid, unimaginative. Too, he has persuaded himself he holds the pearl in trust."

"Yes," Floyd confirmed. "He told me almost the same thing. Still, I'm beginning to wish I'd never laid eyes on the thing."

Crawley, before continuing his tale, found a pack of crumbled cigarettes and offered one to Floyd, who declined, before lighting up with his Zippo. He knew better than to ask Hazzard, who neither smoked or drank alcohol.

"The pearl was lost for a thousand or more years." He exhaled a puff of smoke. "Then an adventurer stumbled across it in a jungle-choked temple guarded over by white cobras! This adventurer sold the pearl to Van Dyke, then died of injuries received in the jungle. He had a daughter. But he left no address of her whereabouts, and Van Dyke has been holding the purchase money in trust for her. He's already spent thousands trying to find her."

As Crawley paused to take another drag, Floyd asked, "How is you know all this stuff, anyway?"

"Fair question," the journalist grinned. "Van Dyke came to me to help him find the missing owner. He figured, aside from the police, a newspaper writer might be a good bet in finding someone."

"Makes sense," Floyd agreed.

"Once Van Dyke explained about the Red Maggot, I spent a few days at the library and did my own research. The stuff I found was incredible, to say the least. Especially its importance to the people of the South Seas."

"How so?"

"The Dyaks and Malays attribute weird things to that pearl. But they are always tied up with murder, greed, unwarranted conquest. That's why some say the Red Maggot should never return to the Malay territories; it would mean revolt. Van Dyke, it turns out, owns a coral island somewhere in the Java Sea, I believe. It has an immense pearl bed there that his people nurse. He also has invented a way to make perfect pearls by some electrolytic process…"

"Are you serious?" the seasoned world traveler was having trouble believing such things were true.

"Very much so," Captain Hazzard took up Crawley's tale, being familiar with the science behind artificial pearls. "With his process, Van Dyke discharges high frequencies through treated sea water, thus killing all impurities. Pearls are made, you know, by some minute bit of grit or foreign matter adhering to the inner side of an oyster or similar shell. Nacreous matter covers this impurity with many layers of 'skin,' which forms the pearl.

"The pearl, created by impurity, often has its value impaired by other impurities."

"Yup, go to the head of the class," Crawley wasn't surprised at all by Hazzard's endless store of knowledge. "Van Dyke told me that was the phase of pearl culture his process had overcome. He can make real pearls with astonishing speed by stepping up the voltage. Hell, if he were a dishonest soul, he could easily ruin the pearl markets of the world..."

"Say, isn't that a fire up ahead?" Thomas Floyd interrupted.

Chapter Four
A Girl in the Road

"I've been watching it for some time," Captain Hazzard stated, voice grim. "I believe it's somewhere close to Eastgate College. Wait, there's a motorcycle scout. Perhaps he can tell us." He pulled up at the curb beside the motorcycle policeman.

The officer threw the beam of a flash on Captain Hazzard, then grinned. "I'd know you anywhere, citizen. You're Captain Hazzard. What can I do for you, sir?"

"What can you tell us about that fire, officer?"

"The fire's in the chemical lab at Eastgate. Two girls were making a dangerous experiment, I hear, and it exploded on them."

He drew a slip of paper from his breast pocket, directed the beam of the flash on it. "One of'em named May Eaton. The other," he peered again at the paper, "was named… Rima Van Dyke."

"Too late!" Captain Hazzard whispered, face taut and drawn. His deduction had proved correct. This chemical lab fire was no accident, but a planned move by some master mind of crime.

Suddenly Captain Hazzard tensed. From afar had come the thin shrill of a woman's scream. Neither Floyd, Crawley nor the motorcycle scout had heard it; so acute was Hazzard's hearing. To their left was an old road which wound around the base of the hill on which Eastgate College was situated. Hazzard knew the area well. Without another word, he quickly meshed the gears, twisted the steering wheel to the left and slammed his foot on the gas pedal. The patrolman watched them race off, puzzled by the famous crusader's reckless departure.

"What are you…" Floyd started to say.

"A scream. Down this old road," Hazzard announced. "This back road circles the college grounds."

The dirt road was rough, full of holes and dips. The solid Cord 812 lurched and bounced, but he kept it moving at a dangerous speed. Floyd and Crawley grabbed whatever they could to keep from being tossed around.

"There, ahead!" Captain Hazzard suddenly cried, and there was a triumphant timber to his voice. "On my side of the road, Floyd! Look, she's waving us down. It's a girl, and she's frantic with fear!"

Captain Hazzard pulled the car over toward the girl, jerked on the emergency brake. He jumped from the car, strode to the girl's side. In the light of the headlights, he saw her distended, fear-crazed eyes, her blonde hair in wild disarray. She held trembling hands to her face, and Hazzard saw her curvaceous body was twitching with fright. Over her dress she wore a long white laboratory smock similar to the hundreds of people who worked for him at Hazzard Labs. She took her hands from her face, held them imploringly toward him.

It was Rima Van Dyke!

"Captain Hazzard! Is it really you?"

"Yes, Miss Van Dyke."

"Oh, Captain, thank God. They… they're after me!" She faltered. "They tried to blow me up with… with a bomb, back in the lab. I escaped and… they saw me run. They started after me and… passed by just a moment ago. I hid behind the bridge approach…

"Heavens, here they come!"

She pointed wildly ahead, turned to run but Captain Hazzard's strong arms puller her to him.

"Floyd, kill the lights!" Hazzard snapped. "We don't have time to get the car off the road. Take the girl and all of you hide behind it."

He handed off the shaking girl to William Crawley, then ran swiftly toward the old wooden bridge, directly into the jumping beam of light thrown by the headlights of the approaching car. As

"... he felt the shock of hot lead close to his running feet."

he ran, Captain Hazzard peeled off the glove from his right hand and then opened one of the pouches on his utility belt.

In a moment, six or eight little glass pellets were in his hand. They were innocent appearing, but within the glass was a terrible corrosive acid that acted instantly. It would eat through toughest steel, sear flesh like a living flame.

From ahead came the sudden rat-tat-tat of a machine gun. Captain Hazzard was twenty yards on the far side of the rickety old bridge now, running low and with amazing speed. He heard the staccato blasts of a .38, saw the flashes of livid flame. But every flash missed in the darkness. Then, the car almost upon him, Hazzard tossed the handful of glass pellets in front of the speeding murder car, arrowed for the side of the road.

The machine gun continued its spiteful yammer, and he felt the shock of hot lead close to his running feet. Then the aim was again changed to his own car outlined in the headlights. The murder car... he saw two occupants as it zipped past... was speeding close to sixty miles an hour even though it bounced dangerously.

There was a dull explosion as a tire blew out. Another followed. The acid pellets had eaten through the tire rubber within the space of ten short yards.

The wheels of death swerved, lurched, slammed the bridge abutment, careened in a mad, grinding half-circle. All was silent for a long second following the crash. Then a dull red eruption of fire spewed into the night.

Captain Hazzard ran forward, but he could not get close due to the terrific heat of the gasoline-fed flames. He ran past, joined Rima and the others on the far side of the bridge.

"I'm afraid they're both dead," he said grimly. "Too bad, they could have told who is behind all this."

"It has to be that strange customer, Nomar Samadi," William Crawley theorized, as they all watched the fire consume and blacken the wrecked automobile.

"What is this all about?" the frightened girl asked Hazzard. She was quickly regaining her composure. He was impressed with her grit.

"There was an accident outside your father's shop earlier this evening."

"An accident." The fear returned to Rima's lovely features. "My father, was he hurt? He was supposed to fly to Singapore this evening."

"Rest easy, Miss Van Dyke," Captain Hazzard spoke softly to calm her. "You're father was not seriously hurt, and from what we've been told, he did leave for the California as planned."

In swift, clipped phrases, Hazzard told the girl of what had transpired at her father's Fifth Avenue store. When he was finished, he introduced his companions.

"Rima, this is Thomas Floyd, who was a witness to the events I've just related. And this is my associate, William Crawley. He is a reporter for a city newspaper." As the two men nodded politely, Hazzard's eyes hardened with an idea.

"I am going to have Bill write up a story and say you are… dead."

"What… me… dead?" she faltered, paling under his steady gaze.

Hazzard inclined his head, taking her into his confidence. "Yes, that you died in the chemical explosion. I've an idea you were to be killed so you couldn't check up on your father. It will serve him best if the one behind this murder game believes the attempt on your life was successful."

"Hot dog!" Crawley exclaimed. "That'll make the front page for sure, Captain. My editor will eat this up!"

Hazzard looked to Thomas Floyd. "Can I depend on you to keep silent?"

The explorer's face beamed with childish delight. "But of course, Captain. I would never do anything to jeopardize the young lady's safety. You can count on me."

"Then we're agreed." Captain directed his attention to the girl again. "I believe you are the only one besides your father who can open the inner safe in which the Red Maggot is kept. If you are up to it, we'll go back to the shop and have a look for ourselves."

He broke off as he heard the sound of the motorcycle speeding toward the red blaze of the burning car.

Captain Hazzard explained to the patrolman what had happened. "Wish you'd have the coroner in this district send anything he finds on the dead men on to my headquarters at Hazzard Labs. Have him also get the fingerprints, if possible."

Those arrangements made, Captain Hazzard and his party returned to his sleek automobile. He got behind the wheel of the Cord, and sixty minutes later stopped in front of the Van Dyke store. Jubal Beck had locked up for the night, but Rima had keys to the front door. Soon she had the larger safe open, was working the combination of the smaller one.

At Captain Hazzard's suggestion, Crawley phoned the airport to learn the complete details of on Otto Van Dyke's movements. He completed the call, returned to the safe where Hazzard was watching the girl.

"Nothing new, Captain," he reported. "Mr. Van Dyke and his secretary left on the plane as scheduled. I was told he seemed weak from exhaustion and all information was given by the secretary..."

Rima Van Dyke looked up, face livid. "Secretary?" she exclaimed. "Why, he never traveled with a secretary in his life! I don't..."

"It's Samadi!" Captain Hazzard guessed. "No one would know your father didn't travel with a secretary if you were... dead! That's one of the reasons you were to be silenced tonight, so that fact couldn't be looked into. I expect Beck also was to be killed. He..."

Hazzard turned as he heard a gasp of dismay from the jeweler's daughter. She pointed in wordless consternation.

Captain Hazzard peered within the inner safe built to protect the Red Maggot. It was empty.

"I thought so," he said quietly. He turned to Floyd. "The form you saw making for the safe in the smoke was that of Samadi. He was doing that deliberately, making you think it was Van Dyke locking up the Red Maggot. In that way there'd be no immediate suspicious the pearl was stolen."

The crime-fighter's smile was tight now, making his lips taut. "Mr. Floyd, I understand you are about to travel to the South Seas on a new scientific venture."

"That's right. I'm going for the Chicago Museum of Natural History to study the coral beds in that part of the world. My ship, the Cora Marie, is even now being outfitted with supplies for the voyage. Why do you ask?"

"Do you have room for additional crew members?"

"I suppose, we haven't signed on a full contingent yet. Who did you have in mind, Captain?"

"Myself, and two of my associates from Hazzard Labs. And Rima, of course?"

The girl smiled, arms folded over her bosom. "You had better believe it. You wouldn't have a chance of finding father's secret island without me."

"I... don't understand, Captain," the puzzled explorer said. "What are you planning to do?"

"I want to give this Samadi character plenty of rope, and then..."

Kevin Douglas Hazzard's jaw was set, his eyes hard as if of frozen agate. Without another word, he led the way from the Van Dyke shop into the cold street.

Outside, Thomas Floyd managed to hail a taxi cab that would take Miss Van Dyke to her Manhattan home and then drop him off at his downtown hotel. The group would meet the next morning at Grand Central Station to board an express train to the West Coast.

As the yellow cab drove off, Captain Hazzard and William Crawley climbed back into the Cord 812.

Crawley was glad to be out of the cold wind. "So, who are you taking with you, Captain? A South Seas jaunt. I sure wish I was tagging along."

"You are far more valuable to me here in the city, Bill." Hazzard started the Lycoming V-8 engine and pulled out into the empty street. "Wash is still working on the few machines we salvaged from Circe's Citadel in Colorado and Tracey is on duty for the next several weeks at the St. Carmel Children's Hospital in Brooklyn."

The reporter nodded. He was aware that Hazzard's cousin, Dr. Martin Tracey, one of the most gifted young surgeons in the country, volunteered several weeks annually to work at St. Carmel's for free. It was a source of much pride to all the members of Captain Hazzard's team, that one of their numbers was such a self-less humanitarian.

"Which leaves..."

"Randall and Cole," Hazzard finished.

"A pilot and a cowboy on a sea voyage in the balmy South Pacific.

That should prove interesting, to say the least."

"Don't discount Randall's mechanical skills, Bill. I've yet to see the engine he couldn't build or repair. And as for Jake, well, he's just a good man to have at your back in a scrape. And something tells me, there's going to be plenty of those before this is over."

Chapter Five
Crawley Comes Through

Rima Van Dyke slowly shook her head at Captain Hazzard's question. "I'm not certain at all," she said. "My father was always secretive regarding the location of Lost Island. It isn't on the Admiralty charts. All I know is that it lies about halfway between the tips of Borneo and the Celebes in the Java Sea."

Captain Hazzard frowned. There were, he knew, scores of tiny coral islands not shown on the various charts of the South Seas. Every once in a while some new one was discovered, so it was not unusual that Van Dyke's island wasn't generally known. He looked out the window of the speeding railroad car. chartered by Thomas Floyd and the Chicago museum.

They were in the lounging area of the first of two private cars chartered by Thomas Floyd through the auspices of the Chicago Museum. He and Rima Van Dyke were seated on padded chairs, while across the aisle, caught up in a game of cards, were Hazzard's men; the tall, blonde pilot, Tyler Randall and the slim, wiry Montana cowboy, Jake Cole. Cole, as ever was wearing boots, dungarees, a leather vest over his shirt, a red bandana around his neck and his ever-present, big white Stetson.

"If it weren't for this run of bad luck I'm having," he proclaimed, losing his sixth consecutive pot to the pilot, "I wouldn't have no luck at all."

Captain Hazzard inwardly cringed at the sharpshooter's disregard for proper grammar. He knew Jake, raised on a cattle ranch in the Badlands, had had very little formal education. It didn't mean he was ignorant, far from it. Behind that small, sharp featured face was a very keen intelligence and wit. It only lacked what society types would call polish.

Cole put a stick of chewing gum in his mouth and began assembling the playing cards. "You want to play another hand?" he asked Randall, who was busy adding the small mound of nickels and dimes to his growing stack.

"Ha," the pilot laughed good-naturedly. "Why not, I've been wanting to get my hands on that ten gallon chapeau of yours for some time now."

"Oh no you don't," the cowboy replied as he shuffled the cards. "I'll bet my pants first before I ever put up my Stetson."

Catching Rima Van Dyke out of the corner of his eye, he blushed and turning to her, tipped that very hat. "Sorry about my language, Ma'am. I didn't mean to offend you."

"None taken, Mr. Cole," Rima Van Dyke assured him. "We modern girls are a little tougher around the edges."

Besides this lounging car and the sleeping one behind it, the museum had funded several baggage cars to hold the personnel and the large amount of baggage, scientific instruments and supplies. The museum's fantail motor yacht, the Cora Marie, was already in San Francisco harbor. The new and improved bathysphere, which was to be used in studying coral growths, was being loaded on the ship at the moment.

Hazzard took his gaze away from the passing vistas out the window. "Who knows the island's location besides your father, Rima?"

"Just two men. Even Jubal Beck doesn't know it, and father trusts him implicitly. Of course Paul Dupres… he's the technical supervisor in charge of the island… knows its location. The other is father's Singapore manager, Jonathan Wells. Uncle Jon, although he's no relation, is my father's closest friend. Paul Dupres is a brilliant scientist and chemist. Those three are the only ones knowing the location of the island outside of two or three government men."

"It would be useless to contact this Jonathan Wells by radio phone for the location," Hazzard mused. "I doubt if he'd tell us anything even if we were face to face. He would have no reason to trust a stranger like myself.

"We'll set out for Singapore via the Java Sea in the Cora Marie. I've already made arrangements with Floyd on that issue. Maybe we can find this island if you're certain it's approximately half-way between Borneo and the Celebes."

She nodded. "But why try to find the island first? Don't you believe Samadi will take my father to Singapore first?"

"Perhaps so. They will go there first if it isn't found out that the death notice I had Crawley write up telling of you being blown to bits in the lab explosion is a fake. If it is discovered you are alive, this Samadi, who undoubtedly knows the location of Lost Island, will hide there. But," he smiled, "you are officially dead. I know of no one outside of this party who is aware that you came through safely, not even Beck."

"Oh, that's for certain," the girl chuckled. "Mr. Floyd whisked me out of my home early this morning, through the backyard entrance where he had a cab waiting. On the drive to the station he had me keep my head down, then he handed me this ridiculous hat," she held up a gray floppy head-piece with a stitched on veil, "and told me to wear it as we ran through the station. It was like something from a spy thriller."

"All of which was necessary," Captain Hazzard said. "Floyd was merely carrying out my directives to keep your identity hidden."

"Oh, I do understand, Captain. Still, it is hard to believe that just twelve hours ago I was being shot at with machine-gun bullets! Now here we are on a train bound for San Francisco and I'm not even sure if I grabbed my toothbrush on my way out…"

"Ah, Hazzard, there you are!" The words came from Thomas Floyd coming into the car from the rear door. He hurried over to them, a folded newspaper in his hands. "I knew you'd want to see this."

Cole and Randall put down their cards and gave their attention to Captain Hazzard as he took the morning edition from Floyd and opened it. Rima Van Dyke was anxious to know what was written there. "It's right there on the front page," the explorer pointed out. "In the middle."

"Please, Captain," the girl begged. "Read it aloud."

"Very well," he adjusted the paper in his hands and then began. "The headline reads, Attempt At Pearl Store Manager's Life with a lower bar that says Jubal Beck Escapes, by William Crawley.

"Paragraph one; Jubal Beck, manager of the New York interest of the vast Otto Van Dyke pearl organization, was attacked by masked thugs en route to his apartment last night. The attack followed the mysterious death of Rima Van Dyke, daughter of the pearl millionaire, who was blown to bits in a laboratory explosion at Eastgate College earlier in the night. It is believed that Otto Van Dyke is present on his way to Singapore via China Clipper, and could not be reached by the authorities.

"Paragraph two; Mr. Beck could attribute no reason for the attack. Two thugs with automatics opened fire on him but the bullets luckily missed. Inspector James Chambers of the Detective Division is handling the investigation."

Captain Hazzard refolded the paper and handed it to Rima. "Crawley did a good job. Anyone reading that will believe you are deceased."

"Thanks, I think." She studied the news account as Thomas Floyd questioned Hazzard.

"If you know this Samadi character is enroute to Singapore, why not radio the authorities there to pick him up when he and Van Dyke arrive?"

Hazzard steepled his fingers and thought for a second before replying. "I had considered that avenue of action last night and discounted it."

"But why?"

"Because it will only net us Samadi and I am convinced he is only a lieutenant in this plot. The real mastermind hasn't yet come into the picture, preferring to manipulate events from the shadows. We have to catch the entire gang of plotters. That the Red Maggot is missing is conclusive proof that revolt against white dominion in the South Seas is the core of the plot."

"Van Dyke said as much in his office last night," Thomas Floyd added.

He moved over to a counter at the front end of the car where a porter had earlier set a plate of pastries and large carafe filled with coffee. "Would anyone like a refill on their coffee, or a pastry? Traveling always seems to increase my appetite."

Both Cole and Randall rose from their seats and joined their host at the counter, bringing with them their empty mugs. "Don't mind if I do," Cole said. "Those little squares with the whipped cream and jelly are mighty tasty."

While Floyd set about pouring the hot java into their mugs, Rima Van Dyke used the opportunity to switch subjects. "There is still one thing I don't fully understand, Captain, and I'm hoping you can resolve that for me."

"If I can."

"What's your particular interest in all this? I mean, I've read about some of your past exploits but they don't make any sense. You aren't really a legal representative of the law, are you?"

"Actually, Rima, I am."

"Really? I had thought your title was some kind of honorarium for past services to the country."

Kevin Douglas Hazzard smiled. "Well, there is that too, but the truth of the matter is, I am a bona fide officer with the rank of Captain by the authority of the Joint Chiefs of Staff and entitled to all the benefits and privileges of that rank."

"I see, but that doesn't explain why you do what you do? What is it the tabloids call you?"

"The Champion of Justice," Jake Cole mumbled around a mouth full of sweets. "And they're one hundred percent right! Ain't they, Boss?"

Thomas Floyd, carrying a fresh cup of coffee, pulled up a chair and set it next to Rima's. "This is fascinating. Please, Captain, I believe Miss Van Dyke is interested in your particular motives and quite frankly, so am I. It isn't every day we find ourselves in the company of a 'Champion of Justice'."

"My story isn't all that exciting," Hazzard explained. "But if you must know, then here it is. I was the only child of a Superior Court Judge in upper state New York. Members of a criminal organization attempted to bribe him and he refused. In fact he went to the police and gave them the name of the agent who had approached him. Unfortunately the police force in that particular town was corrupt and nothing was done about my father's charge.

"I was only a baby at the time. A few days after the incident we were going for a drive in the country. A bomb had been place in the car and when our chauffeur hit the ignition switch, it blew up. He and my parents were killed instantly. As I was still on the curb, in the maid's arms, we were somehow spared. Still the closeness of the blast blinded me and I spent the first fourteen years of my life in darkness."

"My God," Rima responded softly, "what pain you must have suffered."

Captain Hazzard touched the area just over his right eye where the small white scar was visible. "Actually, it was loss of my family that hurt more than any physical suffering. I was taken in by relatives and sent to a school for the blind. My father had left me a sizeable inheritance which my uncle wisely invested on my behalf. By the time I was a young man, I was independently wealthy and would never want for anything.

"Anything, that is, except for justice." A cold, hard look filled Hazzard's eyes. "You see, the men responsible for my parent's murder were never caught or made to pay for their crimes."

"So you've taken on that burden," Rima Van Dyke said, coming at last to some understanding, "as a life's mission."

"Yes, I have dedicated my life to the cause of justice and the destruction of evil. Wherever it rears its many faces."

"What an amazing story," Thomas Floyd mouthed, his coffee getting cold in his hand. He hadn't taken a sip during Hazzard's speech.

"You're a remarkable man, Captain," Rima said. "But I sense you are also a very lonely one."

A small grin touched the corners of Hazzard's mouth. "And you are a very perceptive young lady."

Otto Van Dyke sat with unseeing eyes, his face turned toward the window of the China Clipper. Underneath was the smoothly rolling Pacific, glinting under the rays of a horizontal sun. He seemed in a trance. The pupils of his blue eyes were pinpoints. When his eyes moved they jerked. His face was expressionless, showed no interest in the huge flying boat or the fact it was flying over the ocean.

Seated next to the pearl millionaire was a tall man with eyes of coal black. Occasionally his red lips curled wolfishly away from hi startling white teeth. It was Nomar Samadi. He narrowly inspected his companion's face with his cruel eyes. Then he pressed a button at the side of his seat. A steward came up, listened attentively.

"My employer would like a glass of orange juice," Samadi said.

Shortly the steward returned but as he turned away he did not see the bit of white powder Samadi dropped into the liquid. Van Dyke drank the juice at Samadi's command, doing it obediently as would a sick child.

The radio officer hurried toward Samadi and handed over a radiogram. There was pity on his young face. Samadi read the words on the radiogram, frowned in the presence of the officer.

"Would you like to send a reply, sir?"

Samadi leaned closer and spoke softly so only the radio operator could hear: "Mr. Van Dyke is too ill, as you can see, to learn of the terrible death of his daughter at this time. It could cause him much harm."

"I understand, sir."

"Please advise all who know of this message that he must not learn of its contents."

The radio operator nodded, his face again filled with pity. He returned to his post. Samadi sat back, folded his hands over his stomach and closed his eyes. All was going smoothly according to plan.

Chapter Six
The Cora Marie

When they arrived in San Francisco two days later, it was a lovely sunny day temperatures in the low 70s. A far cry from the from the frigid winter weather back East. It was almost noon and several of the Cora Marie's crew drove two old flatbed trucks to the loading docks to help pick up all their cargo. They were quickly introduced to Manuel Ramirez, a gray-haired, pot-bellied Mexican; the ship's cook and steward, and Hank Carter, a tall, rugged fellow with tattoos covering his bare, beefy hams. He was Floyd's First Mate and Navigator.

With the help of Captain Hazzard, Cole, Randall, and a few paid porters, all their gear was successfully loaded onto the two trucks. It was decided Rima Van Dyke would ride with Thomas Floyd in the first truck being driven by Carter, and Hazzard and his men would follow along in the second with Manuel at the wheel. As they started to leave their train car, the explorer picked up the outlandish veiled hat and held it up to the lovely blonde.

"Oh, not again," she said frowning. She looked to Hazzard with pleading blue eyes. "Do I have to?"

Captain Hazzard shook his head, "It really is for the best, Rima. We can't take the risk of anyone seeing you. Of course this won't be necessary once we're out to sea."

"Oh, very well." She yanked the offensive hat from Floyd and pulled it over her head. "Never let it be said I wasn't a team player."

The ride through the city to the harbor was uneventful and Hazzard allowed himself the luxury of enjoying the ride through the beautiful City by the Bay. He had been to San Francisco many times but it never failed to captivate him with its old world feeling, it's trolley cars and steep, climbing hills.

At the harbor, the rest of the crew was waiting to help bring Thomas Floyd's scientific equipment and personal items aboard. First Mate Carter took charge of the detail, allowing Floyd to lead his new friends down the wooden planks of the wharf out to the slip where his ship was anchored.

An afternoon sky was dotted with a few puffy clouds in a clear blue sky filled with soaring gulls calling out their shrill greetings. The smell of brine was everywhere and Captain Hazzard relished the sight of the water. When they came upon the long, fantail yacht, Thomas Floyd opened his arms up like a symphony conductor and waved them out to the long, beautiful vessel moored before them. As Hazzard stood admiring the motor ship's clean lines and her twin decks, Tyler Randall came up beside him and whistled, "Weeeyooo, Captain, she's a beauty."

Floyd heard the comment and his smile threatened to split his face in half. "That she is, Randall. That she is. The Cora Marie is my pride and joy. She's one hundred and seven long with a beam width of twenty-two feet. She's powered by twin Detroit diesels and can do 8 knots cruising, 9 knots at max."

"How much water does she displace?" the savvy mechanic asked.

"Exactly two hundred and ninety thousand pounds."

As they continued to approach the lowered gangplank, the explorer continued to brag on his new vessel. "Miss Van Dyke, you'll be happy to know your accommodations include three double staterooms, two with en suite heads, one having been prepared for you, cast iron bathtubs, and five single cabins with bunks.

"The main deck features a full dining room, galley, main saloon with fireplace. The aft deck has been customized as a work area for our diving operations. You can see our bathysphere {3} secured there beside the portable crane to lower her into the water and then retrieve her."

Through the lace veil, Rima's eyes were wide with awe at the magnificent craft that would be their home for the next few months. "She is truly an elegant ship, Mr. Floyd. I can hardly wait to get aboard."

The euphoric Floyd swept off his fedora and extended his arm over the gangplank. "Then wait no further, my friends. Welcome about the Cora Marie, one and all."

As the party made its way across the wobbly plank, they acted like children on Christmas morning, eager to discover what new toys had been spread out for them. As Randall and Cole came up behind Captain Hazzard, each toting a huge, dark green duffel bag, Thomas Floyd addressed the tall pilot.

"Mr. Randall, if you'll put your bag down and join me at the bow, there is something there I think you'll appreciate."

Randall did as the ship's master suggested and, with the others, trailed Floyd along the side deck to the ship's bow. There they found something mounted dead center of the bow, covered by a huge canvas tarp. "If you'll give me a hand removing this," Floyd indicated the tarp as he reached to take hold of one corner. Tyler Randall grabbed the other end and together they peeled away the sheet from what sat beneath.

"Hot dang!" the cowboy yelled out, excitement in his cry. "It's a small airplane!"

Indeed, sitting astride a steel catapult bolted to the teak wood deck, was a light weight, fixed winged aircraft with fat engine cowling behind its single propeller. Although it was a short, stubby looking contraption, its struts fitted into two pontoon floats and the cabin suggested she had room for three, with two seats forward and one in the rear.

Randall jumped up one of the catapult braces and running his hands along the fuselage, looked through the pilot's side window at the instrument panel, the steering wheel and elevator and rudder control pedals fixed on the floor. There was much to admire about the construction of this little seaplane. At the tip of the nose, where the engine cowling began, was the painting of a yellow, cartoon bee, its wings vibrating, its feet covered in pontoon shoes.

{3 **AUTHOR'S NOTE:** A bathysphere is a hollow ball of steel used for underwater exploration and scientific research. The greatest danger of a bathysphere is that it might develop a leak and the weight of the water pressure cause an implosion – the opposite of an explosion. It must be remembered that Dr. William Beebe descended to a depth of 3,028 feet on Aug.15, 1934 in the ocean six miles south of Nonsuch Island, one of the Bermuda group.}

"We call her SeaBee," Thomas Floyd said coming around from the tail and looking up Randall. "What do you think if her?"

"I think I'd love to take her up, Mr. Floyd."

"Well, you just might get your chance, Randall. You see, it was the museum's idea to add her to our ordinance. Our travels take us to many out-of-the-way places where we could easily find ourselves marooned and out of radio contact with the outside world.

"The SeaBee is a solution to such an emergency contingent." Thomas Floyd could not help himself patting the little plane just as Randall had done.

"All this work, bracing the area below deck to support the SeaBee and her launch catapult was all done during the past few months. We were about to go looking for a skilled pilot to join our crew when all this happened."

Captain Hazzard climbed up on the other side opposite Randall, his own appreciation of flying machines evident in his eyes. "Mr. Floyd told me about the SeaBee and I told him he needn't look any further. That you'd be only too glad to fill that position while on this voyage."

"And then some," Randall said without hesitation. He dropped down to the deck and stuck out his hand. "You've got yourself a pilot, Mr. Floyd."

Thomas Floyd laughed happily as he shook the big man's hand. "Excellent. It seems like everything's starting off on the right foot. Although, I do think that now we are aboard the Cora Marie, it's only fitting all of you stop calling me Mr. Floyd and start using the more appropriate seagoing title of Captain," he looked up at Hazzard, "...or Skipper? Wouldn't want people being confused with two captains on board, would we?"

Tyler Randall grinned and whipped off a salute, "Aye, aye, Skipper!"

Floyd clapped his hands. "Wonderful. Wonderful. Now, let's get cracking, put our supplies aboard and cast off. The South Seas await, gentlemen."

Three hours later, with all their gear stored, and crew squared away, the Cora Marie, slipped out of her berth with engines purring, sailed through the Golden Gate and into the mighty Pacific Ocean. As her bow cut through the purple-blue waters, the guests were all on deck watching landmass fall away behind them.

The Skipper emerged from the pilot house, his pipe in hand, wearing a jaunty captain's cap, a turtle neck sweater and bell-bottom trousers. Spotting his friends, he came down from the upper deck to join them.

"What is that land formation in the distance, to the right," Rita Van Dyke, now free of the cumbersome hat, inquired pointing.

"Those, my dear, are the Farallon Islands. Nothing much there but some rocks and a Coast Guard light house. Oh, and allow me to instruct you in naval terminology. Right on a ship is starboard. Left is port, then there is fore and aft."

"Fore and aft?"

"Fore being the front, the bow of the ship. The aft is the back end more commonly referred to as the stern."

"Thank you, Skipper. I do think you'll make a sailor out of me yet."

"What is our setting?" Captain Hazzard asked, enjoying the taste of the salt-air in his lungs. It smelled of adventure.

"Due south for most of the night," Floyd replied, starting to pack tobacco into his pipe. "We'll reach the Channel Islands just about dawn and from there turn due West, South-West."

Chapter Seven
Bombs Farewell

The sky was lightening with streaks of pink and orange across a dull gray-blue horizon as the sun crept up behind the Cora Marie, at dawn the next morning.

Unable to sleep, her mind awash with excitement and worry for her father, Rima Van Dyke came up through the deserted lounge and passed the galley on her way to the aft deck. She caught a whiff of coffee brewing and looked forward to her first breakfast aboard. Nothing like the salt air of the open sea to build a healthy appetite.

Coming out the panel doors, she realized she was not the only early riser. Someone was moving to the right of the bathysphere, in some kind of practiced ballet. As the ship's fantail was now facing east, light from the rising sun blinded her and Rima had to shield her eyes to make out who it was.

A few steps closer, the wind blowing her blond tresses playfully, she recognized a naked Captain Hazzard. Or so it looked until her vision cleared and she saw he was wearing tan swimming trunks and rubber-soled boat shoes. He appeared to be doing some kind of slow-motion dance routine. The girl stood still, not wanting to disturb him as he went though his odd motions, at times raising his legs, waving his arms and twisting his body, always in a graceful flow.

A blue-blooded, American college girl, Rima Van Dyke couldn't help but be swayed by the near physical perfection of the man she watched. Tall, lithe, with tanned muscles stretched across a flat stomach, and with that Clark Gable mustache and those dark, icy-blue eyes, he was the dream she, and all her sorority sisters, secretly harbored. A beautiful hunk of manhood. Inwardly she laughed, oh, how green with envy would her friends be if they could see her now, sharing a sea voyage with the famous Captain Hazzard. Remembering their conversation on the train, she wondered if he'd ever been truly in love. Was there a woman in his life? She couldn't help wonder what kind of woman it would take to turn his head? The foolish imaginings continued until she began to picture herself in his strong, powerful arms...

"Good morning, Rima, it's a lovely day." His voice shattered her sexual fantasy and startled her back to reality. He had stopped his odd dance and was using a towel to wipe sweat from his face and arms.

"Oh, excuse me, Captain," she stammered awkwardly, praying she wouldn't blush. "I didn't mean to intrude on your... ah... ah.."

"Exercise," Kevin Douglas Hazzard supplied. "It's a very old Chinese form of exercise called Tai Chi. It tones the muscles of the body at the same allowing you to free your mind in a gentle, meditative state."

"Fascinating. Would you teach me, I mean, if we have the time?"

His smile returned. "I don't believe free time is going to be a problem for the next couple of days. And yes, I'd be happy to teach you Tai Chi."

The buzzing noise came up from behind them and they turned to look skyward, again into the bright white-hot glare of the climbing sunrise.

"What is that?" she asked, moving next to Hazzard, who was also shielding his eyes with his hand.

"An airplane," he answered, all too familiar with the steady humming of airplane engines. It was getting closer.

True to the Skipper's orders, the Cora Marie, had turned westward just before daybreak and was now moving through the Channel Islands that dotted the coast of Southern California. When he was able to make out the airplane, swooping down at them from out of the sun, he assumed it had come from one of the inhabited isles.

The plane was a Curtiss JN-4, better known as Jenny. Built by the Curtiss company of Hammondsport, NY, she was one of the most used trainers in the years prior to World War One. Captain

Hazzard had learned to fly in a JN-2 long ago. As the bi-wing plane descended upon them, he saw the twin-seater was occupied, with goggle wearing fliers in both the front and rear cockpits. Maybe one of the islanders was taking a flying lesson, he thought as the sound of the Curtiss OX-5 inline engine buzzed louder as they drew nearer.

Then, just as the Jenny was coming up over them, the man in the front cockpit lifted his arm out and Rima began to return what she assumed was a friendly wave. Captain Hazzard's keen eyes saw the man was holding a metallic object and as the Jenny banked, he released it. Following its path, Hazzard recognized the elongated egg-shape with the tiny fins on its tail.

Captain Hazzard grabbed Rima and dove to the deck, rolling them under the steel shell of the bathysphere just as an explosion to port sounded with a water-deadened boom and a spray of water splashed over the side.

"Oh, my God!" the girl gasped, wide-eyed with fear. "That was a bomb!"

Captain Hazzard couldn't waste time confirming the girl's statement. Not when the Jenny, seeing she had failed to hit her target, was banking around in front of the yacht and starting to come around for a second pass.

Instantly on his feet, Hazzard pulled the blonde up and pushed her toward the saloon doors. "Find Jake Cole fast and tell him we need Old Betsy! He'll understand!" As Rita Van Dyke disappeared into the main cabin, Captain Hazzard bolted along the side deck to the steps leading up to the pilot house. These he took three at a time and came barging into the small, cool, room where the first mate, Hank Carter was helming the wheel and looking very, very upset.

"What the blazes just happened out there, Hazzard?"

"There's an airplane overhead dropping bombs on us! The first one exploded just off our stern by only a few feet."

"What?"

Hazzard pointed out the window to port. "Look for yourself! She's coming around again to drop another one!"

Both men saw the plane's long fuselage as it swooped past them, still a good distance away.

"She's going to try and come up our stern again, and hope to hit us square amid ship."

"Like hell they will!" Carter cursed and gritting his teeth began spinning the giant wheel to starboard as fast as he could." "Nobody's sending us to Davey Jones' locker without a fight."

"That's the spirit!" Hazzard slapped Carter on the back. "Just keep going back and forth like that. Don't give them a decent target."

"Aye, mate. But we can only zig-zag for so long!"

"I know," the crime-fighter agreed as he started out the door. "Just give us a few minutes and leave the rest to me!"

Hazzard exited the wheel house in time to see the Jenny diving for another run at them. Thomas Floyd was just coming out onto the deck followed by other members of the crew. All of them were frantically looking about, trying to determine what had caused the explosion that had rocked them.

"GET DOWN!" Hazzard yelled, his voice booming over the sounds of the diving Jenny.

Once again he saw a hand triggered bomb falling towards them as the old plane swept over. At the same time he felt the entire hull cutting into the swell to a hard starboard. Would they make it? The small missile of destruction hit the water again, only yards away and detonated.

The Cora Marie was jolted and several of the crew knocked off their feet as another gusher splashed over her sides. Hazzard thought she might have taken some damage along her waterline.

Grabbing the handrails, he slid down the stairs to confront a very furious Thomas Floyd. "What the bloody hell is going on here?" the Skipper fumed, rising to his full height. He looked past Hazzard's shoulder into the sky at the retreating aircraft. "Who are those madmen?"

"Most likely more of Nomar Samadi's people. Do you have any guns aboard?"

"Of course we do. There's an armory below."

"Then break out your rifles and let's give our flying friends a proper reception."

Floyd wasted no time in following Captain Hazzard's advice. Meanwhile Rima Van Dyke appeared at the stern accompanied by

Jake Cole and Tyler Randall. Cole was dressed only in his worn Levis and his ten-gallon Stetson, while he swung a long, Sharps buffalo rifle in his hands. Randall had on cotton pants, boat shoes and a black tee-shirt.

"You wanted Ole Betsy?" the cowboy said, hefting the Sharps. "Here she is, Chief. What do yah want me to shoot?"

Captain Hazzard pulled the cowboy to the railing and pointed past the bow to where the Jenny was starting to climb. "I want you to get up on the roof of the bridge and take out her engine when she flies over. Did you bring the flare-rounds?"

Cole reached into his pants pockets and pulled out a four extra long, copper bullets; each packed with a mixture of gunpowder and magnesium.

"Right here, Chief."

"Good, get going!"

Grabbing his hat tight on his head, Jake Cole started forward at a fast clip. He would take the stairs to the wheel house and from there climb out onto the roof.

"What can I do?" Randall wanted to know, clearly eager to get into the action.

"The Skipper is getting rifles from below. As soon as he comes out, position his men on either side of the ship and get them ready to lay down a barrage."

Suddenly the ship shifted to port without warning and all of them had to grab the deck railing before being flung over the side. Hazzard smiled. Carter was giving her one hell of a work out.

"Here she comes again!" Rima called out, pointing back to the Jenny.

Thomas Floyd and his men emerged, all wielding Enfields. As Randall started orchestrating them into defensive positions, Captain Hazzard dashed into the now empty lounge. He heard the airplane pass overhead and the sharp pop-pop of rifle fire. But this time there was no accompanying explosion. Carter's turn to port had come at just the right second, causing the airplane to over-shoot the Cora Marie and make dropping another bomb futile.

He knew they only had minutes before the attack would resume. There was no way of knowing just how many of the hand-primed explosives they were carrying. Which was why he had to move fast. As the entire scenario was playing out in his mind, Captain Hazzard had been devising strategies at the speed of thought. Then he remembered something important. The Jenny's pilot continued to come at them from astern, clearly using the glaring brightness of the sun to his advantage. Then again, that very ploy could easily be turned against him. Hazzard saw the object he was after and went for it.

Jake Cole threw back the hatch and climbed onto the roof of the pilot house. The ship rocked up and down beneath his feet like a bucking bronco and he felt right at home. Balancing himself carefully, he searched the skies for the enemy flier. There she was turning to starboard this time, arcing around in a long, easily maneuver. Whoever the pilot was, he was clearly experienced with the dependable JN-4's stick.

Hurriedly Cole tightened the Stetson chin chord around his neck, flipping the big hat over his shoulder and out of the way for what he was about to do.

He pulled the slide back on the Sharps and inserted one of the flare-rounds and slapped her back into the chamber. Wiping his forehead with the back of his hand, he hefted the famous Western rifle to his right shoulder and set about sighting over the barrel. He aimed the Sharps to the rear of the Cora Marie, from where he knew the aircraft would be coming. Immediately the sun's glared shone in his eyes and he had to turn his head away.

"Darn it!" he mumbled to himself. "That varmint is one cagey hound dog, coming in out of that sun like that."

"Maybe I can help with that," Captain Hazzard said, poking his head out from the still open hatch. "Here, Jake, grab hold of this and be careful with it."

The cowboy looked down in delightful surprise as his boss handed up a good-sized wall mirror with ornate gold framing. He immediately recognized it from one of several hanging in the expansive lounge area. As he took hold of it with one hand, keeping the Sharps in the other, Hazzard pulled himself up and onto the roof beside him.

Before straightening, he called down to Carter, "Alright! Now keep her steady! No more bouncing around!"

"Aye, aye, mate. Steady as she goes!"

Taking up the mirror, he said, "Thought we should fight fire with fire."

Cole knew instantly what Hazzard was planning to do and laughed. "It should do the trick, Chief. Like my daddy always said, what's good for the goose, is good …"

"Here he comes!" Tyler Randall yelled from the stern.

"Get ready!" barked Hazzard. "You're only going to get one good shot at this."

Cole brought the Sharps up and began to line up with the colored flags whipping off the stern jib line. "Let 'em come! Ole Betsy and I are all ready to give him a nice, warm howdy."

A half dozen rifles began firing. The drone of the 90 horsepower engine swelled and Jake Cole squinted, just making out the dark blur coming out of the giant white orb that was the sun. "I see her, Chief!" He took a deep breath, and put his finger on the trigger, the barrel riding upward.

Standing to Cole's right, Hazzard held up the heavy mirror to chest level and began to canter it towards the sunlight. It lit up as the sun's rays met the shiny, reflective surface. Having captured the sun, Hazzard tilted the powerful glare towards the sounds of the Jenny's motor.

The aircraft was almost over them when the white beam from the mirror hit the cockpit and Hazzard's sharp ears could hear two very startled cries. Then the aircraft wobbled slightly and the nose dropped several feet as she flew over them.

Cole continued to track the aircraft, then, as it was passing directly overhead, he squeezed the trigger. Blam! The flare-round smacked into the engine and a loud, metallic shriek ensued. Black smoke began spilling out of the cowling and the pilot frantically pulled the stick back to get them in a climb to safety.

"You got them!" Captain Hazzard exclaimed, as he put the mirror down, his gaze staying with the now damaged Jenny.

"I ain't done yet," Cole said as he ejected his spent shell and chambered a second round. "I can still put another one in her belly!"

In their short years together, Captain Hazzard had seen the

"Get ready!"
Hazzard barked.

Montanan do some amazing shooting. At the moment, he had absolutely no doubts as to the veracity of the cowboy's claim. He watched in admiration as Cole swiftly took up a firing stance, aimed the powerful rifle, swung his arms up a bit more and then fired. The echo over the waters was barely fading when Cole's bullet plowed into the undercarriage of the aircraft and continued up through the pilot's body. Hazzard saw the tiny figure's arms flail and then his plane began to roll over. It quickly became a downward spiral, with flames now consuming the front fuselage. The bomber in the front cockpit was attempting to climb free of the doomed flier. He didn't have a chance.

The wounded Jenny hit the water, the impact igniting whatever remaining bombs were still aboard. She blew up in a massive fireball, the concussion blasting at them from a quarter mile away.

Twenty minutes later, Skipper Floyd held a meeting in the salon with Rima Van Dyke, Captain Hazzard, Randall, Cole and First Mate Carter.

"So, Captain," he began. "What do you think that was all about? Did our foes somehow uncover our subterfuge regarding Miss Van Dyke's being still alive?"

"Unlikely," Hazzard said, his demeanor cold and serious. "If you'll recall the article Bill Crawley wrote, these people, believing her dead, still launched an attack on Jubal Beck. No, I think whoever is behind this was directing this particular attack at you and me. It seems clear they do not wish us to proceed any further."

"You mean they don't want us to find this so called Lost Island?"

"That would seem the only logical conclusion."

Everyone let Hazzard's words sink in, fully aware of the horrible fate they had barely avoided thanks to his quick thinking and Jake Cole's remarkable marksmanship.

"But Captain," Tyler Randall followed Hazzard's hypotheses to its natural conclusion. "When those two birds in the Jenny don't report back, their leader is going to know they failed to stop us."

"That's right!" Thomas Floyd piped up. "What happens then? You think they'll come after us again?"

"I don't know," the champion of justice replied. "But I suggest, for the remainder of our voyage, we remain on constant alert and vigilance."

"Agreed," the ship's master nodded. "Carter, I want you to set up a twenty-four hour security detail. I want at least two members of crew properly armed and on guard duty at all times."

"Aye, aye, Skipper, I'll get right on it."

As the sailor departed to fulfill his assignment, Jake Cole, who was next to the lovely blonde, leaned over and whispered. "When you travel with Captain Hazzard, ma'am, there's never a dull moment."

Rima thought it was the most outrageous understatement she had ever heard.

Chapter Eight
Forty Fathom Fight

"**Y**ou say this island alee isn't on the Admiralty charts?" Captain Hazzard the question of Hank Carter, the chief navigator on the expedition. The First Mate shook his head. Hazzard looked through the prism binoculars at the towering coral cliffs of an island to starboard.

The trim motor-yacht had made the trip under forced draft due in large part to the fully equipped machine shop and laboratory below decks. These facilities made it possible for Thomas Floyd and his crew of trained technicians to carry on experiments even while at sea.

For the past two days now, the Cora Marie had beat up and down the Java Sea on a line with the tips of Borneo and the Celebes. Now, after hours of search, an island of pinkish coral lay to starboard. Captain Hazzard was certain it was Van Dyke's Lost Island, the location of his fabulous bed of virgin pearl shell and the plant for manufacturing pearls.

Captain Hazzard, face taut, stood with Floyd and Carter by the giant steel ball and explained what he wanted to do next. "We're alee of the island and there's no sea to speak of, so it's time to employ the bathysphere. Has she been air tested?"

"Yes, I saw to it personally," Skipper Floyd said with pride. "I don't believe the sea bottom here is deeper than forty or fifty fathoms. We'll drop our sea anchors as close as possible to those coral cliffs there. What do you hope to find, Captain?"

"Some physical proof that this is Van Dyke's Lost Island."

Carter clapped his hands at two of the deckhands. "You two mind the lines and I'll personally man the phone, Captain."

"Good, then let's get away before we waste any further daylight."

Within thirty minutes the sea anchors were in place fore and aft, and the Cora Marie was stationary alee of the exotic coral island, its cliffs only fifty yards away. The electric fathometer recorded bottom at approximately forty-two fathoms. Captain Hazzard, again stripped down to his bathing trunks and boat shoes, walked to the raised platform on which the bathysphere sat.

The bathysphere was, like its name, cylindrical. To its top was affixed a steel rope fastened to a lowering drum. The telephone and air lines were played out with the steel rope with which the bathysphere was raised and lowered. The interior of the large ball was fitted with numerous scientific instruments, auxiliary oxygen tanks, and had accommodations for four divers. While under water it was possible for a portion of the sphere to open and allow egress to the floor of the ocean.

Within this pressure chamber were three diving suits, which could be donned while in the bathysphere itself. Then, by means of the inner controls, water allowed to enter the pressure chamber until conditions outside the bathysphere were reached. Followed the opening of the hermetically sealed door and the diver was ready to carry on explorations with the bathysphere as a base for replenishing air.

The new diving suits were self-contained. It was not necessary for cumbersome life and air lines to be attached to them; the oxygen was fed to the heavy shoulder plates. Enough oxygen was stored within the small tank to allow a diver to live for an hour away from the bathysphere. A reserve supply good for ten minutes was stored in a small cylinder attached to the larger one.

Machinery below deck raised the bathysphere's platform several inches to a rail bar on which the ball would slide into the ocean from the rear of the fantail, held and guided by steel cables. As Captain Hazzard climbed into the steel ball, he gave a wave to his friends gathered around. Randall and Cole stood to either side of Rima Van Dyke, an anxious look on her pretty face. Although dives in bathysphere had become routine among oceanographers, they were still considered dangerous.

Earphones clamped to his head, Captain Hazzard gave directions through the fixed mouthpiece at his lips. The steel door was securely clamped, the air working perfectly. He glanced out the thick, quartz window and could see his friends a few yards away watching anxiously. Hazzard closed his eyes and touched his forehead, silently sending the tall blonde pilot final instructions. Keep an eye out for any trouble, Randall. If this is Van Dyke's island, there may be more of Samadi's men around.

He opened his eyes and saw Tyler Randall giving him the thumbs up signal at the same time he mentally received, Will do, Captain. Jake an eye will keep a sharp eye on it.

That settled, Hazzard checked the various instruments to make sure they were all functioning properly. Everything looked ready to go. He spoke into the mouthpiece.

"Lower away! Stop at three fathoms for inspection."

The automatic wench began to slowly unwind the steel cable. The bathysphere slid into the water and began to sink, shortly stopped.

Inside the huge ball, Captain Hazzard nodded with satisfaction as he inspected the various gauges and tested the flow of air. Everything was in tip-top shape and the champion of justice gave crisp orders into the telephone.

"Lower away slowly. At thirty-eight fathoms let rate of descent be extremely slow. I'll tell you when I touch bottom. Stand by!"

The bathysphere resumed its controlled descent to the ocean floor. From the fused quartz portal located over his control panel, Captain Hazzard saw a myriad of brightly-hued tropical fish flash past. Sunlight, he knew, would penetrate many fathoms through clear turquoise waters, allowing him to view the wonders of underwater life.

Ahead of him lay a deep shadow, undoubtedly cast by the coral reef. A pilot fish darted past, and Hazzard grinned. Somewhere in his wake he knew a shark must be swimming, probably eyeing with displeasure this strange trespasser in its domain.

At last the sinking motion of the bathysphere ceased. Captain Hazzard peered at the depth gauge, saw it registered thirty-eight fathoms. The top-side gang, under Mate Carter was doing a very efficient job. Then the steel ball slowly settled. He felt it grate against coral, flashed the signal through the telephone. The bathysphere gently rested on the bed of the Java Sea.

Captain Hazzard put his eyes close to the window of the metal diver. Outside it was dusk, but the water remained clear and he could see dimly for yards in any direction. The huge steel ball had settled in a bed of growing coral fashioned in fantastic shapes. Everywhere on the seabed were huge oysters, mussels, giant clams. Like a forest of tiny trees, rose the brilliantly colored coral growths.

But it was the shell that interested him. He could see this bed of virgin shell had not been molested. Here, he assumed, Otto Van Dyke recovered some of his most valuable pearls. No wonder the cautious German didn't want the location of this island to become known! Here, within reach, was the tremendous fortune in pearls of the finest water, worth riches of a rajah.

Captain Hazzard's main purpose in making the dive in the bathysphere was accomplished. The dive proved this was Van Dyke's island, for the pearl bed was as the old German had described it to William Crawley.

Had he chosen to abandon his war on crime, Kevin Douglas Hazzard could have stood high in the realm of science. The bathysphere, to his trained perceptions, was simple enough. He had amazed Thomas Floyd on several occasions, during the voyage, with his insightful comments on ocean biology. Although this was his first dive in a bathysphere, he had many times been underwater in a regulation sea diving outfit.

Now he was determined to get into one of the suits with which the giant ball was fitted and venture out onto the floor of the ocean. There was a reason for this, one that was yet vague in his subconscious.

A private smile on his expressive lips, Captain Hazzard entered the pressure chamber, took one of the diving outfits from its hook. He struggled into the heavy suit, the act made easier by his lack of clothing, saw that the oxygen tank was in order. Then he lifted the helmet in place, clamped it. The air flow was a bit slow so he opened the valve wider. Then he screwed shut the bathysphere door, opened the valves which allowed sea water to enter the diving chamber.

Every detail of the intricate mechanism worked perfectly. Within five minutes, the pressure approximating that of the outside, Captain

Hazzard pushed open the door. Through it he saw the wide reaches of coral, the semi-opaque word of water. He stepped from the steel ball onto the ocean's bed.

And then, inexplicably, Hazzard's body became as motionless as the shadowy coral cliffs. His amazingly receptive mind had received some precognitive flash of menace from this waste of water and coral growth. He turned his head within the helmet, peered in all directions.

He took a step forward with ponderous slowness. Again the feeling of imminent danger, of some unknown, deadly force close by, filled him. But there was no fear in his mind. He again stepped forward, his dark blue eyes glazed with the wintry enamel of grim purpose.

To his left a fish suddenly darted like a streak into the shadows. Hazzard turned. An involuntary cry of surprise escaped his lips. He thought at first it must be some strange reflection in the water, some concoction of his mind.

But his mind was too well disciplined for imaginary figures to be imprinted there. There could be no mistake, no error.

Advancing toward him, a long, keen stabbing knife held menacingly in front of his body, was another diver!

Slowly, methodically, the attacking diver advanced. The knife was held rigidly forward, the point out to stab into Hazzard's rubber diving suit. He knew that should the blade penetrate the tough, rubberized fabric, the sea water would rush within the air-inflated suit, cause his death by drowning.

And then Captain Hazzard did the unexpected. Unarmed, he advanced to meet the murderous foe making for him!

The mysterious diver hesitated. And in that moment of indecision, Hazzard stepped within range of the stabbing knife. The diver lunged forward. Hazzard parried the thrust, stepped to one side and threw the weight of his body and the heavy suit against the other.

The enemy diver slowly fell back. In another instant Captain Hazzard twisted the knife from the man's hand, dropped it. The other struggled to regain his footing. Hazzard tried to step forward, but something was clamped around his foot. He looked down.

The shell of a giant clam had closed on his foot, held it as firmly as if it were within the cruel jaws of a bear trap.

Then, with amazing swiftness, millions of air bubbles swirled and eddied the, caused a blanket of white to curtain the unknown diver's form from Captain Hazzard's eyes. Swiftly, the bubbles disappeared. Hazzard blinked and stared. The other diver had vanished.

While above the surface, aboard the Cora Marie, Tyler Randall felt a vague alarm in the furthest reaches of his mind. He pulled Jake Cole away from the others and whispered in the cowboy's ears, "The Captain's in serious trouble!"

"How in tarnation do..?" then Cole remembered the pilot's telepathic abilities to communicate with their chief via thoughts alone. "Oh, yeah, right. How bad is it?"

The somber look on Randall's face was enough to make Cole stop chewing the wad of gum in his mouth. "Darn! What can we do?"

"Nothing, Jake. I'm afraid whatever is happening down there, the Captain is on his own."

Chapter Nine
Death Strikes in Mid-Ocean

Taut lips shut above a square jaw, Captain Hazzard gazed down through the murky water at his foot held by the giant clam. He was aware that often pearl divers were caught by these huge mussels – held so firmly it was impossible to break loose – there to drown.

Hazzard surveyed his predicament, nodded as he saw the long stabbing knife he had wrested from the villainous diver. By stretching his length horizontally among the coral growths he was able to touch the knife with his finger tips. Finally he reached it, slowly toiled upright once more.

The knife was a sturdy one, was firmly embedded in a haft of bone. Hazzard attacked the tough muscles of the bivalve which held its shell closed. The pressure on his foot decreased and he was able to withdraw it.

His face, wet with sweat from his efforts, broke into a momentary smile. Quickly he retraced his steps to the dangling bathysphere, entered the pressure chamber.

It was not necessary to undergo a long period of decompression so, five minutes later, he switched on the valve which blew the sea water from the diving compartment. The diving suit was replaced on its hooks. He grabbed the microphone and signaled Carter to raise the bathysphere.

A few minutes later, Captain Hazzard saw the face of Hank Carter peering anxiously at him through the fused quartz window. He nodded, smiled. In a moment the door of the huge ball was unclamped and Hazzard stepped to the deck of the yacht much to the relief of his friends and associates.

"What happened down there?" Tyler Randall asked, handing his employer a terry cloth robe.

"Aye, mate," Carter joined in. "What caused all those air bubbles earlier? We thought for a moment an air coupling had worked loose. It worried…"

Then the first mate looked in through the door and saw the still dripping diving suit. "Hells bells! You didn't say you were going out in a diving suit! We couldn't reach you for about ten minutes on the telephone and began to think it was busted."

Thomas Floyd, standing behind Carter couldn't contain himself a minute longer. "How'd the apparatus function, Captain?"

"Splendidly, Skipper," Hazzard said while smiling at the tense face of Rima Van Dyke. One of the sailors gave him a glass of water and he drank it greedily.

Something was in Captain Hazzard's mind now that he hadn't had time to think of while below. As he finished his drink, he began to mentally relay his experiences with the attacking diver to Tyler Randall. At the same time this allowed him to see the one fact he missed during all the action below.

What is it? Randall mentally inquired, after Hazzard had finished his play by play account of his underwater combat.

There has to be an underwater entrance to Lost Island!

There had to be. No other ship was in sight, so it stood to reason the unknown diver had walked from within the island upon seeing the bathysphere make its dive. What deadly menace was now afoot? It seemed all too clear now that Lost Island was in the hands of No-mar Samadi and his men! Hazzard continued sharing his thoughts with his pilot.

"Skipper! Skipper!"

All eyes on deck turn to see the radio operator running towards Thomas Floyd waving a piece of paper in his hands. The explorer took the yellow sheet and his eyes narrowed as he read it at a glance. His lips came together, made a thin line across his rugged, sunburned face. He beckoned to the girl and she came to him, her face showing white.

"I'm sorry, Miss Van Dyke, but I've just received some bad news concerning your father. This message is from Singapore. It is a public news flash my radio man just picked up."

"What does it say?" the girl asked bravely. "You can tell me straight out."

Captain Hazzard, Randall and Cole crowded in around the pair, adding their support to the girl they'd all come to admire and respect.

"Your father is very ill from some strange malady," Floyd went on, compassion in his words. "He's in a hospital but the doctors are baffled with the case. I'm so sorry to have to tell you this."

"You should go to him without delay," Captain Hazzard advised.

"Oh?" the distraught girl cried, her face ashen. "It... would take many hours in the Cora Marie. He may... die... before..."

"Captain Hazzard was thinking of another way to get you there," Floyd explained knowingly. "He wants to fly to Singapore. Right, Captain?"

"With your permission?" Hazzard said. "We could be there in half the time."

"By all means, sir. Go at once, with my blessing."

Rima stood on her toes and impulsively kissed Floyd on the cheek, causing it to redden. "Oh, thank you so much!"

Captain Hazzard slapped a hand on Tyler Randall's arm. "Make ready the SeaBee, Randall! You will be coming along as co-pilot."

"Yes, sir!"

Hazzard turned to the blonde. "Go and change your clothes and be ready in fifteen minutes. We are going to fly you to your father."

As they all went about their various assignments in preparation for the flight, Captain Hazzard thoughtfully reviewed the events of the past few hours. He was in his cabin dressing, his mind calculating all the time what their next move should be against a very wily and deadly opponent.

There was more than compassion for Rima Van Dyke in his decision to fly to Singapore. Lost Island was indubitably in the hands of Nomar Samadi's forces. Otto Van Dyke, in all likelihood, had served his usefulness to the gang, now was to be done away with. Captain Hazzard had no doubt that Van Dyke's strange malady was nothing but the effect of some virulent poison.

Thus, taking the girl to her father would serve another purpose. If the German merchant was in a Singapore hospital, then Nomar Samadi was not far away.

Captain Hazzard strode into the pilot house where he found Thomas Floyd, puffing on his pipe and keeping company with First Mate Hank Carter. Beyond the helm, he could see Randall, with Jake Cole's help, loading the SeaBee.

"Gentlemen," he nodded. "It is my firm belief that Nomar Samadi's men are sequestered on that island."

"What!?" Floyd almost lost his pipe when his mouth opened. "How do you know this, Captain? What proof have you?"

In a few short sentences, Hazzard related his battle with the mysterious diver and his assumption of how the fellow had reached him. "I didn't want to say too much in front of the crew," he added. "It would have only scared them unduly. But I did take Randall and Cole into my confidence."

"What do you want us to do?" Floyd asked, unable to take his eyes off the rocky cliffs of the now ominous island before them.

"For the time being, nothing. In fact it would be best if you acted as if you were unaware of their presence altogether, at least until I return. In the meantime keep your men armed and don't let your guard down for a second.

"If Samadi's men don't think you pose a threat, they will most likely leave you alone for the time being."

"I take it this mercy flight isn't just to reunite a father and daughter, then?" Skipper Floyd was a smart man.

"Correct. It is my hope that Samadi himself will be in Singapore and I can apprehend him there."

"Then good luck to all of us," Thomas Floyd wished sincerely as he and Captain Hazzard shook hands.

They moved out onto the deck and made for the catapult on which sat the SeaBee. A detail of the ship's mechanics swarmed over it, saw to the fuel supply – its power plant was a Diesel engine of high horsepower – emergency rations, flares, a medical kit and a score or more things with which it was equipped. Captain Hazzard personally installed near his seat a small box of light steel construction.

The SeaBee was a three-person amphibian, fitted with a huge radial motor, a new type reversible-pitch steel propeller, and was constructed wholly of a light weight alloy.

There was a burst of quick power from the special Diesel motor, and Randall, in the co-pilots chair, indicated that all was in readiness. Jake Cole placed three small bags in the luggage compartment behind the rear passenger seat, then reached down and taking Rima's hand, helped her aboard with a sly wink before jumping back onto the deck. Captain Hazzard climbed in and took his at the controls. The motor was revving up smoothly, showing the necessary rpm's. Hazzard switched on the silencer a moment, said to the girl:

"Put your head back against the headrest. A catapult take-off is a rather strange experience, but it lasts only a few seconds. Just lay your head back and relax. Ready?"

Face strained and white, she nodded.

Captain Hazzard was a devoted aviator and kept pace with the tremendous development in aviation and flew all types of ships. In his hangars at Hazzard Labs he maintained his own fleet of familiar and unique aircrafts; among these were the single-seater Z-2, the Sikorsky S1-38 Seaplane and the powerful, twin-engine Silver Bullet with its experimental rocket booster. He flew these and his amazing dirigible, Argonaut, queen of the clouds, on his adventures throughout the world.

Hazzard, eyes glued to the temperature gauge, knew the rpm of his steel prop was at the 1,700 mark. He raised his hand and a crewman at the catapult's controls pressed a button. There was a dull explosion followed by the hiss of compressed gases. The catapult boom slid forward and literally threw the SeaBee into its element.

Jake Cole whipped off his cowboy hat, waving it over his head, cried out, "EEHAH!! You ride her, Captain!"

The little plane shot away from the Cora Marie, dipped a moment, and then the Diesel motor took up its throaty cadence of power. The plane lifted, circled the yacht once, then pointed its whirling propeller due east. In seconds it was but a dot above a waste of water that was the Java.

Rima Van Dyke, after her initial fear, relaxed and seemed to enjoy the flight, although Captain Hazzard saw little gray ghosts of worry deep in her blue eyes. He surprised her several times gazing at him, wondered why she averted her eyes so quickly when he turned, why faint flushes of crimson touched her cheeks.

It was mid-afternoon now and the SeaBee drummed along at a steady 250 mph. Hazzard and Randall had long ago set the Sperry gyroscopic robot pilot, lounged in their seats. From next to his seat, Tyler Randall brought out a package of sweet biscuits and a thermos jug of pineapple juice.

Suddenly Hazzard, keen eyes shaded against the glare of the sun, caught Randall's arm and pointed below. Far away on the horizon lay a streamer of serpentine smoke. He got out his high-powered binoculars.

"It's a tramp steamer, Randall. Seems to be en route to Singapore like us. But here, look almost beneath us! There's something in the water that attracted my attention. Wait, I'll swing us around so you can have a better look."

He disengaged the robot controls, banked the plane in a turn to port. He straightened out at Randall's yell of surprise.

"It's a life raft, Captain! And there's somebody in it! How in the world did that tramp steamer miss seeing it?"

"That could be easy enough," Captain Hazzard said crisply. He pushed forward on the control wheel, gently closed the throttle. The whistle and shriek of wind came to their ears as the SeaBee spiraled downward toward the choppy surface of the water.

Fifty feet above the breaking waves, Hazzard opened the throttle once more, cruised in a tight circle around the life raft. Suddenly his eyes narrowed and puzzled astonishment parted his lips.

The person in the dirty white raft was alive, and incredibly, it was a girl!

Captain Hazzard made a perfect landing in a long swell of water, brought the nose of the plane about and blasted the tail around. In another ten seconds he was as close to the raft as possible. He unlatched the cabin door on his side, turned to Randall when half out of it.

"We'll have to leave her behind us with the baggage. She appears unconscious, but I don't think she's been exposed much to the sun yet. At least her skin doesn't show it. Looks to be Chinese from here." Hazzard had a sudden inner image of Circe Yu Sun and shrugged it off. "I'm going after her."

With those words, Captain Hazzard dove into the water cleanly. Rima gave a little cry of fright as his head vanished from sight. With two powerful Australian crawl strokes his fingertips touched the bobbing raft. A quick upward lunge brought him aboard.

As it turned out, the girl who lay supine before him was not Chinese. From her attractive, exotic features, he surmised Eurasian. Her slightly long, oval face was the color of very light amber, her lips red, her cheekbones high. Hair black as obsidian was parted in the center, lay close to her shapely head. She wore Chinese costume, the knee-high slit of the glow disclosing a shapely leg encased in gossamer hose. She was alive, for the steady rise and fall of her full bosom could be seen under the thin Shantung silk of her gown.

And then she opened her eyes. They were a deep slate-gray tinged with little flecks of gold. Her eyes slanted ever so little, lent a sensuous touch to her appearance that made her rescuer blink. He smiled down at her.

"You're all right, now. I've a plane here. You are to come with me. You'll soon be safe in Singapore."

"Singapore?" she asked. There was a melodious tinkling sound to her voice, and Hazzard was reminded of the little silver bells hung in the Musical Pagoda in old Peking.

"Yes, Singapore," he repeated. Then: "Can you swim?"

She shook her head negatively.

"We'll have to swim back to the plane. You can trust me to keep your head above water. Will you do it?"

The girl sat up and look around at the water and then the SeaBee. "Yes, I will try."

"Good girl. Slip into the water when I tell you, put your hand on my shoulder. Now!"

With those directives, Captain Hazzard slid into the water, turned toward the girl. She crawled to the edge of the raft. Her gold-flecked eyes studied him momentarily. Then, as if placing her confidence in him, she let her lithe body be drawn into the warm water. He felt the heat of her slim fingers on his shoulder, could detect no tremble. She was a brave girl. Hazzard headed toward the seaplane, using his left arm for the stroke. He looked at her and smiled reassuringly.

Captain! Behind you! Came the mental warning from Randall. Sea snakes!

Hazzard lifted his head slightly and could see Tyler Randall leaning from the cabin window, pointing frantically. Behind you, sir! Poisonous sea snakes!

Upon the instant, Captain Hazzard went into wild action. He knew of the poisonous sea snakes infesting the waters of tropical oceans. The yellow-bellied sea snake, particularly, was feared. It is a slim killer hardly two feet in length but it is akin to the cobra, having a bite that is deadly.

And, Hazzard saw, Randall was right. He and the Eurasian girl were ringed about by deadly sea snakes, and even as he watched the circle grow smaller, cutting off their avenue of safety to the amphibian. {4}

Captain Hazzard saw something else now that brought a momentary frown of dismay to his face. The SeaBee had drifted during his rescue of the girl and was now a good fifteen yards away. He had to go on as the sea snakes were between him and the life raft.

The frightened girl gave a low cry of horror. Apparently she knew and feared sea snakes. Her slim arm went about Hazzard's neck, and he felt it tighten, almost cut off his wind.

"Don't!" he commanded in a low, tense voice that stung here like the lash of a bullwhip. "Get behind me, put a hand on each shoulder. Quickly, or it will be too late!"

Gasping, the girl did as commanded, but Captain Hazzard felt the hotness of her breath on his neck. With fingers moving so rapidly they seemed a blur of action, he dug into one of the many pockets of his utility belt. His hand reappeared, and in it was a plastic bag containing a number of small tissue-wrapped packages.

He tossed one of the packets behind him into the very thick of the sea snakes. Another went to his right and left, two in front of him. Almost instantly a white steam rose off the surface of the water followed by a furious boiling. The effervescent acid in the dissolving packets halted the attack of the sea snakes, burned their bodies.

As the dying snakes twisted about in a frantic attempt to escape the burning water, they cleared a small path before him. Now with powerful strokes, Captain Hazzard flung himself forward, crossed the dis-

{4 **AUTHOR'S NOTE:** The blow-gun, or sumpitan of Borneo is between six and seven feet in length and made of ironwood. The arrows used, all of them envenomed with poison, are about ten inches long, pointed with fish-teeth, and feathered with pitch. Fair accuracy is gained for distances up to sixty yards, and at twenty to forty yards the aim is deadly.}

tance to the Seabee and threw the girl onto the pontoon. Tyler Randall was there to take hold of her and in another instant Hazzard was safe beside both of them. There was no sign left of the sea snakes.

"Gosh!" was all the tall pilot could say. He wiped dripping perspiration from his face, heaved a great sigh of relief. "That was too close, Captain."

Hazzard nodded, agreeing. "Help me get our guest into the plane."

Tyler Randall grinned, the command bringing him out of his terror of a moment before. Between them they helped the girl climb into the cabin to a spot behind the rear seat in the luggage area. Rima Van Dyke was ready to help the lovely survivor get settled and comfortable, as was humanly possible in the cramped cabin.

Captain Hazzard bent over the controls, fed fuel to the motor. After a hundred-yard bumpy run over the roiling waves, he had the SeaBee on the step, pulled her into the air. He adjusted the robot control, turned and looked at the Eurasian girl seated on a small box to Rima's right.

"Well, how did you get on that life raft, miss? You might tell us your name, too." His smile was open and friendly.

"My name is Azlea, Azlea O'Hara. That name should mean something to this girl and you – Captain Hazzard!"

Hazzard started. Now he knew this girl being on a life raft in the Java Sea was no accident. It meant that Samadi's gang knew everything, was leaving no stone unturned to stop them.

Captain Hazzard smiled and tugged his chin as he saw the puzzled faces of Tyler Randall and Rima Van Dyke. He looked straight at the exotic beauty.

"Well?" he asked softly. "What's the rest of your story?"

A sneer was now in Azlea's voice as she daggered a look at Rima. "My father was Seamus O'Hara, the adventurer who found the Red Maggot and sold it for a handful of gold to this girl's father! Now you are helping her, trying to keep the Red Maggot from returning to the Malay territory where it rightfully belongs.

"Yes, this was all a plant. A radio message from Lost Island told us you were bound for Singapore by plane. That tramp steamer you must have seen put me on the life raft so as to lure you to stop. Captain Hazzard," her tone was edged with steel, "you are going to turn

*"Turn back or I'll shoot you!
Death means nothing to me!'*

us around and return to Lost Island! There, you and your friends, will meet the fates you deserve – death!"

Hazzard blinked. With a quick, lithe movement, Azlea O'Hara had drawn a small object from some concealment on her dress. He saw a square of oiled silk on the floor at Azlea's feet. The next second Hazzard was looking into the muzzle of a small automatic.

"I say again, Captain, turn back!" Azlea rasped. "Quickly! The South Seas are for those who live here, not you white interlopers! Turn back, or I'll shoot you! Death means nothing to me!"

Captain Hazzard purposely laughed in her face.

The Eurasian girl, a scream of fury on her red lips, jerked up the automatic and her finger tightened on the trigger. A shot made a vicious spat of sound in the tiny cabin of the plane. Something like white hot steel creased Hazzard's cheek. He heard Rima scream, saw Randall's startled face.

Again her finger squeezed the trigger.

Chapter Ten
Pall of Green Death

C aptain Hazzard's practiced counter-moves for self-protection were impossible in the tight quarters of the speeding amphibian. Ordinarily he'd have seized the tiny, palm-size anesthetizing gun from one of the many pouches of his leather belt. But it was in plain view as he sat, swiveled around to face the gun-wielding, desperate beauty.

But while his right arm was visible draped over the back of his seat, his left was busy behind his back. With quick movements he disengaged the robot control, quickly brought his left knee up to make contact with the control wheel.

A split-second before the Eurasian girl fired again, he drove his knee forward. The SeaBee dived with a lurch that caused her to vibrate horribly, falling seaward with a speed that threatened to shear the stubby wings from the fuselage.

The violent maneuver slammed Azlea O'Hara against the ceiling of the cabin. Rima reached out and caught her, as the gun fell to the floor. She saw in a quick glance that Azlea had been knocked unconscious by the impact.

Meanwhile, as Hazzard turned back to the controls, Tyler Randall leveled the plane, reached for the throttle. Strangely the motor was ticking over, and Randall had to dive again to regain flying speed. Then they both saw what had happened. The enraged girl's second bullet had smashed the throttle segment and Randall could not feed enough fuel into the Diesel engine.

They would have to set her down to make the necessary repairs to the throttle.

Captain Hazzard flashed an anxious glance downward and a taut look overspread his face. They were no longer over the Java Sea. Below was a blanket of undulating green. It was jungle. Then Hazzard knew where they were. It was Borneo.

A forced landing here would mean their deaths, for as far as the eye could reach there was nothing but the pall of green. It meant death, a horrible death. But there was no alternative.

On board the Cora Marie, Skipper Thomas Floyd was pacing the deck of his ship, his lit pipe clenched in his teeth. Over on a make-shift hammock, the cowboy, Jake Cole, was stretched out and snoring away. It infuriated the explorer that the man could sleep at a time like this. Every so often Floyd would stop his marching and look at the foreboding island to starboard. Where Samadi's men really there and watching them even now? It gave him pause.

A wild yell of excitement came from a member of the deck crew and he pointed to port. "Look – the sea's on fire!"

The Skipper led a rush to the rail. Twenty yards away from the yacht a huge column of flame spewed up from the water, leaped fifty feet straight upward!

"Is that some kind of underwater volcano?" Jake Cole materialized at Floyd's side like a stage magician, fully alert and awed by what he was witnessing.

Floyd shook his head. "Impossible here. That fire is made by some human agency. I'll swear to it."

"Look!" the cowboy pointed. "There's a metal can of some kind near the column of flame. I'm betting that there fire was set to draw our attention to that can."

Skipper Floyd called to his First Mate. "Mr. Carter, I believe it wise we raise the sea anchor and move farther from that accursed island. But first send a boat crew for that can and bring it to me."

"Aye, aye, sir," Carter snapped crisply. He yelled out orders and port boat crew jumped to their stations. Soon they were in the water rowing to the floating can, careful to avoid coming to close to the fire.

The boat crew returned presently with a metal container such as refined spices are packed in for shipment. It was tightly sealed, but the ship's carpenter pried off the lid.

Inside was a message typewritten on a square of rice paper. It was addressed to Thomas Floyd. As the Cora Marie raised anchor and began to pull away from Lost Island, he pulled Cole to the furthest end of the bow and read the words softly so no one else would hear but the two of them.

"Thomas Floyd.

It is known to us that Captain Hazzard has enlisted your aid to suit his personal designs. The column of fire you saw a moment ago could have been used to cut the bottom out of your ship. Let it be a warning to you.

All of you will die if any report is made of this island or what happened here. By the time you read this message, Captain Hazzard will be dead."

Floyd stopped reading and took a long breath. Jake Cole was a quiet as a stone statue, a look of pure resolve on his lean features.

The Skipper held up the note again.

"The Red Maggot is to remain in the South Seas and help deliver this territory to the people it rightly belongs to. Beware! Should you return your ship will be destroyed."

There was no signature on the note.

"It's a lie," Cole finally spoke, his voice hard. "Don't you believe those skunks for a minute, Skipper. There ain't no way this pack of sea going varmints could ever get the drop on the Captain and Randall."

"But how can you be sure?" the leathery faced adventurer wanted to believe Cole; to share the cowboy's unyielding conviction.

"Because I know the Captain, sir. If here were truly gone, my gut would tell me so."

"I see," Floyd said skeptically. "So, what exactly is your... ah... gut, telling you, Jake?"

"Well, sir, it's not all that clear. You see, I've got this here feeling, and it's a strong one, that the Chief and Randall are still breathing. But... well..."

"Spit it out, lad. What is it you sense?"

"That they're in one heap of trouble, sir. One mighty big heap of it!"

★★★★★

Captain Hazzard, eyes glazed, shot a glance behind him and saw that Azlea O'Hara was still unconscious. Next to him, Tyler Randall held the rapidly sinking plane as steady as he could.

The plane glided earthward in a long, slanting circle. Now the tops of dark green trees were swishing the pontoons. In another ten seconds the staggering plane would trip on some treetop branch. It would somersault over and over and crash, throw them through the metal plates of the fuselage, crush their bodies to a bloody pulp.

And then he saw it. A ribbon of dirty water, moving sluggishly between narrow banks of hanging vines and drooping jungle growths.

"Randall. Up ahead, a river!" he cried out.

"I see it! Not a whole lot of room, Captain!"

If they could break through the overlapping branches of the trees they would be safe. But just then a new peril threatened.

Hazzard saw brownish rapids dead ahead and beyond, leaping water which told of submerged logs or rocks. But ahead of that was a stretch of smooth water.

"There!" He pointed to the flat water. "It's our only chance!"

Tyler Randall needed no further urging. "Hang on, Captain! I'm going in!" He dipped the SeaBee through an opening in the overhang branches hardly large enough for the plane. But there was no crash, no jar. Randall had made it! Then the flying ace pulled the wheel back into his lap. There was a mighty splash, and water leaped up about them. The plane slowed, came to halt.

"Great job!" Captain Hazzard said with a tight grin. There was admiration showing in his dark blue eyes as he surveyed the man in the co-pilot seat. For his part, Tyler Randall released a heavy sigh, grinned and released the wheel.

Hazzard turned, smiled at Rima Van Dyke, looking none too bad for the ordeal. Azlea, he saw, was conscious now and was studying him with sullen eyes. She offered no excuse, no apology, sat silent, but Hazzard saw that inwardly she was boiling with baffled rage.

"We can stretch our legs a bit on the pontoons," Captain Hazzard suggested. He helped Rima down but Azlea refused help and climbed down with a little strength that brought a look of admiration to Hazzard's face.

"I think we're on the Barito River, Randall," Hazzard said as he watched the aviator work on the jammed controls.

They were in the middle of the sluggish stream, hardly moving with the current. A hundred feet away, on both sides, was the green of the impenetrable jungle. Out there, Hazzard felt were strange enemies in the shapes of wild beasts, deadly poisonous snakes. Unfriendly natives, too, who perhaps had never before seen the face of a white man. Armed with long sumpitans – blowguns –they were eager to aim their poisoned arrows at any trespasser of their jungle fastness.

The green of the jungle, in all shades from a light green to the darker and deadlier hues – engulfed them. It was everywhere, sinister, deadly, a pall of green living, clutching death. As Captain Hazzard's eyes flashed from side to side he saw a sudden movement in a tree whose branches dipped into the water.

As first he saw nothing. Then his keen eyes caught an incredibly long shape, a triangular head. It was a Regal Python, the largest constrictor snake known. It reminded Hazzard of the huge anacondas he'd encountered in Guatemala the year before. This particular python was the dreaded Ular-Sawa of the Malays.

Without moving, Hazzard's penetrating gaze went along the curtained bank of the Barito. He felt, rather than saw, menacing and deadly life there. Then a movement of a hanging tree branch attracted his attention. Again at first he saw nothing save the brilliant verdant colors of the growth, the glistening moisture emanating from the haze of heat rising from the water.

But now something was taking dim ship and form on the retinas of his blue-gray eyes. And then, in startling reality, he saw clearly. It was a Dyak, one of the natives of Borneo, and in his hands was a

{5 **AUTHOR'S NOTE:** This was one of the sea snakes, family Hydrophidae. Quoting from Dr. Raymond L. Ditmars, Curator of Mammals and Reptiles, New York Zoological Park : "They (sea snakes) are for the most part, of striking coloration and provided with fangs and venom so virulent, their rank must be among the most deadly of the poisonous snakes." Again : "The Yellow-bellied Sea Snake is widely distributed. It is common in the Indian Ocean, the waters of Malaysia and the tropical and semi-tropical Pacific waters of the Malay Archipelago, Sea Snakes may be seen swimming in schools of several dozen individuals. My friend, Mr. Rudolph Weber, informs me that when nearing the coast of Sumatra upon one of the regular steamers, he was treated to an interesting spectacle. The sea appeared to become suddenly alive with brightly-banded snakes swimming in every direction in graceful lateral undulations." The poison of these snakes is almost identical with that of the cobra.}

long sumpitan! {**5**}

A splash of water near the pontoon drew his gaze. The snout of a river crocodile showed momentarily and then sank from sight. Captain Hazzard saw other ripples, made out the dark bodies of the beasts ringing the plane. He knew that should one of them fall into the river there would be a concerted rush, a terrific fight...

A tiny movement against the leather of his cavalry boots caused him to look down. Now Hazzard's eyes were narrowed to grim slits. For embedded in his boot was a slim arrow of bamboo. At the point was a dark brownish substance, thick and viscid. Curare, the deadly poison with which the Dyaks tipped their sumpitan darts!

Captain Hazzard's voice was urgent: "Randall, get the two girls in the cabin. Quick! Dyaks with sumpitans are on both banks. I think they are about to send a volley of poisoned arrows at..."

"Looks like we're a little bit late, Captain," Tyler Randall responded.

With those words a piercing war cry split the stillness. Wild birds screamed, shooting off into the sky while monkeys chattered. Hazzard looked up. From up and down the muddy Barito he saw war canoes heavy with painted Dyaks push away from the banks, make for the SeaBee. Other yells added to the din.

These came from Dyaks hidden on the banks on both sides of the river. Again water splashed, and a monstrous crocodile raised his ugly snout, bellowed a challenge. There was sudden quiet. Then a deep voice called out some fierce command.

Captain Hazzard's eyes grew hard. He stepped forward to protect the two girls, but they were on the opposite pontoon. There was nothing he could do. Scores of poison-tipped sumpitan darts were arrowing at them from all sides!

In a moment they would strike, and then the swift virulent of the curare would bite and gnaw at their hearts...

Chapter Eleven
Great Magic

Rima and Azlea screamed as they saw the tiny shafts of death arcing toward them. Hazzard and Randall, stony eyes hard, watched the poison-tipped missiles in flight. The Dyaks, eager for the kill, had badly miscalculated the distance. The little winged deaths fell short, made tiny jets of water leap upward as they fell harmlessly into the Barito.

The towering, blonde pilot jerked his automatic from its holster, made ready to fire, but Captain Hazzard's sharp command held his finger from pressing the trigger.

"Wait," Hazzard said softly. "I can make them understand me. Meanwhile you get into the cabin. We're headed up the river. Work on the throttle. When I give the word start the engine, it may frighten them. Pass down that little steel box in my map case. But first give me a chance to placate them."

"Alright, Captain," Tyler Randall always obeyed orders. "Look, they're coming over."

"That's the chief in the leading canoe. See his headdress," Hazzard pointed out. "The wizened small fellow beside him is his witch doctor."

"How do you know that?"

"The feathered staff in his hands. It's a magic stick."

Captain Hazzard held up his hand and gained the attention of the natives while Randall climbed into the cabin and passed down the flat steel box. Something in his fearless presence stopped the second command to fire from the chief. Hazzard knew that all savages, living as they do in daily physical danger, admire courage in their enemies. The canoes were only twenty-five yards away now, and even with yammering machine guns they would be mowed down by a cloud of poisonous arrows from sumpitans.

"Tabe," Hazzard said easily, addressing the chief.

The leader of the jungle Dyaks looked surprised at being addressed in fluent Malay. He studied them and the seaplane, and the witch doctor leaned over whispering to him. The proud chief stood erect in the bow of his canoe.

He was short, slight, the feathered headdress adding a full foot. His skin was a deep cinnamon brown. Around his waist was a bark loin cloth, and on it hung two hideous dried heads. He held a sumpitan in his hand and attached to his loin cloth was a small cylindrical tube of bamboo.

In that tube, Captain Hazzard knew was the arrow poison in which the tiny shafts were dipped before being blown through the sumpitans. Around his neck was a triple necklace of crocodile teeth, yellowed with age. In his jet black hair were braided small colored gems and the feathered bonnet was a collection of bright hues denoting his elevated position as the chief of his kampong, or village.

"It is not a good day, as you say, white stranger, when you trespass in the land of the jungle Dyaks. We allow no one to come here – and return! Shortly my warriors will reach you with their sumpitan darts and your heads will adorn the ridgepole of my house. You are devil -- devils. So says my witch doctor, and Rapa is wise in these things." The chief pounded his chest. "I am the great M'La, chieftain of all this land. Even the Nedderlanders and the Inggris have fear of M'La."

Captain Hazzard answered him in swift Malay. "We mean you no harm, great chief. Our api tambangan – airboat – came down to rest for only a few minutes. Shortly we shall leave and our coming will bring good fortune to your kampong. But I warn you, great M'La, do not act on the advice of Rapa, your witch man, or great harm will befall you and all your people!"

"Rapa's magic is powerful, poeti oragn – white devil – and he has but to raise his hand and a hundred sumpitan darts will quiver in your flesh."

"I too have magic, great M'La," Captain Hazzard raised his right hand, palms out. It was a stage magician ploy of simple misdirection.

As he has been talking with the natives, fingers of his left hand had delved within the little steel box and when they reappeared, they were clutching a small cylinder of light metal now cleverly hidden behind his back. With a dramatic flourish, Hazzard dropped his right arm and whipped the left out, holding out the metal object for all to see. "Ask Rapa if he knows magic such as this?"

Captain Hazzard flung the small canister in to the air. As he did so, however, his fingers pressed down on a concealed button. A red balloon blossomed at one of the cylinder. The tube was filled with a highly compressed gas. The pressing of the button released it into the large red balloon. Having tremendous lifting power, the gas filled the balloon and it rose into air, growing larger as it ascended over all their heads. Hazzard smiled at the awed faces of the Dyaks. Several of the warriors threw their hands in front of their faces, as if the balloon was some kind of weapon about to attack them from above.

Suddenly the balloon burst with a tremendous noise, and a cascade of red, green and blue fire erupted from the cylinder. It was a "star bomb" such as is fired on the Fourth of July. But to the simple Dyaks it was a major miracle. There were gasps of fear from the Dyak ranks, and they looked uneasily toward M'La and Rapa.

Laughing softly, Captain Hazzard reached down and jerked the little bamboo arrow from his boot. He held it aloft so all might see. Then, with a quick movement, he jabbed it into his naked forearm!

Rima cried out in horror. The Dyaks gasped, looked at each other with wondering faces. Hazzard chuckled again. He was adept at sleight of hand, having learned several tricks from none other than Chandu the Magician. So quick had been his movements that no one saw the steel pin he had taken from his utility belt, and palmed. Then, holding it so as to make a wound, he jabbed it into the top of his arm. It appeared as if the poison-tipped arrow had drawn the blood.

He held up his arm so all could see the blood. Then, contemptuously, he tossed the sumpitan arrow into the Barito directly in front of M'La's lead canoe, again palming the steel pin.

A maddened voice came from behind Captain Hazzard. He swerved, eyes glazed in wintry hues. It was Azlea, and she was addressing the Dyaks in Malay, trying to incite them into attacking!

"It is only trickery, M'La," she denounced. "This man is trying to win more of our islands for his cruel people! Look at me! Hear me! I am native to the Malays although my father was white. This man is your enemy! Have you not heard of the mera mata hari – the Red King – the great pearl-heart known to the foreigners as the Red Maggot?"

Captain Hazzard was tempted to shut her up by forcefully carrying her back into the plane but decided against such action. Better to let her have her say, then answer each allegation calmly with the truth. He had already impressed the natives, hopefully the Eurasians vehemence would not sway them completely.

"Truly, I say to you," Azlea jabbed a finger at Hazzard, "this man wishes to keep the Red Maggot from returning to the Malay States so they, not you, may conquer the dominions of the former colonialists! Attack, M'La – attack!" Azlea, screaming defiance, leaped into the muddy Barito and swam with graceful strokes toward the chief's war canoe!

"So you can swim now! Hazzard said under his breath. He looked at M'La and the shrewd Rapa, saw they were ready to renew their attack. The girl had succeeded in rousing them to action after all. He dug into another of his belt pouches, and with a sweeping motion, he threw something into the bow of M'La's advancing boat.

It was a pellet of thin glass, and within it was a spoonful of acid similar to that which he had used on the tires of the murder car near Eastgate College. The glass shattered against the floor of the canoe, and a burst of sulphurous yellow smoke flew upward in the very faces of M'La and his faithful witch doctor.

Almost instantly the acid ate through the wooden bottom. A wild yell of fright screamed from a score of Dyak throats. Other canoes darted in to save the chief and his warrior crew.

And then, in the utter confusion of the rescue, a piercing female scream of utter terror knifed the thick jungle air. Captain Hazzard swung about and a cry and gasp of surprise escaped his lips. The scream had come from the swimming Azlea. She was only ten yards away from the SeaBee, still on Hazzard's side, but within several feet of her was an immense river crocodile, its reptilian orbs beady, its huge mouth opening to snap at the helpless girl. {6}

Another splash sounded as Hazzard's muscular body sliced into the water in a clean knife dive. He swam underwater with powerful strokes, came up beside the terrified Azlea. His strong hand got the girl by her black hair. He unceremoniously jerked her from the path of the monstrous creature, pushed her backward with a mighty lunge of his shoulders.

Then Hazzard's knife hand came above the water, seemed to dart almost into the mouth of the crocodile. But none saw the tiny ball of glass shatter against the bony structure of the saurian's upper jaw. Before Captain Hazzard dived from view, the inert body of the girl in his arms, he saw the deadly acid take effect.

The crocodile coughed, bellowed, spewed out a cloud of foul smelling, sulphurous smoke. Its terrific death movements roiled the muddy water, caused brown spray to cover the awe-stricken Dyaks.

Brief seconds later Captain Hazzard threw the body of the unconscious Eurasian beauty onto the pontoon of the plane, clambered up himself and carried her to safety. He turned, gazed at the silent Dyaks.

M'La, Rapa and the Dyak warriors had been hauled aboard other canoes, had watched the rescue through staring eyes. Suddenly Hazzard heard gasps of wonder, saw the Dyaks pointing down stream. He followed their pointing arms with his gaze and a satisfied smile hovered about his taut lips. The dead crocodile, white belly upward, was floating down the sluggish Barito. It would soon be torn to shreds by its own kind, such is the law of the jungle where kill or be killed is the law of survival.

"Do you believe now, oh great M'La," he asked firmly, "that I too have much magic? I mean no harm to you or your kampong. The foolish girl's words were a lie. I only wish to go eastward in peace. I want your friendship, great M'La, I want to tell the chiefs of the far cities that in M'La they have a noble friend, one who courteously treats all visitors with the welcome he would expect in their lands. Tell me, great M'La, shall it be peace between our peoples or – war?"

{6 **AUTHOR'S NOTE:** River crocodiles have been recorded to reach 30 feet in length in Malaysia, and 16 to 18 feet is considered common. The crocodile takes a terrible toll on native life each year.}

Voice faltering, cinnamon-brown face working in fear, M'La once more rose to his feet. In the flowery language of the Malays he told of how he had desired peace but for the ill-advised urgings of the wicked Rapa. He - M'La – would see that Rapa was punished for the indignities offered the man-who-was-not-afraid-of-the-river-beasts. And, too, M'La wished to give a present to the white warrior to prove his true change of heart.

Now resolute, M'La commanded his Dyaks to paddle close to Captain Hazzard. His hand disappeared for a moment within his loin cloth. He held something out to Hazzard, who accepted it with a grave bow. In return he gave M'La a metal mirror, and the Dyak chief looked at it in mingled wonder and gratitude.

Captain Hazzard looked down at the hard object M'La had placed in his hand. His eyes narrowed and low whistle escaped his lips. It was an uncut ruby the size of a small egg!

The Dyaks stayed close to the SeaBee as Tyler Randall tinkered with the fuel feed lines, discovered that all was in working order. The two girls were ready in the rear of the cabin. Hazzard wound up the inertia starter. The Diesel motor caught. Its roar of power startled the Dyaks, but Captain Hazzard explained they had nothing to fear. M'La cleared a pathway for the take-off, warning his small fleet out of the way. Hazzard grabbed the wheel, waved farewell through the window, gave the ship the gun.

It was a narrow take-off, the river confined as it was by overhanging branches and trailers of green vine. The Seabee's wings brushed against the tops of jungle trees as it soared into the late afternoon sky, its silvery prop again boring into the east. Captain Hazzard put the ship on its course, adjusted the robot control.

A sad noise of strangled sobbing came to him. He turned around and a sympathetic frown curved his lips. Azlea O'Hara was sobbing, her delicately oval face buried in her hands. As her shapely shoulders under her silken dress began shaking and trembling, Rima Van Dyke sat beside on the floor and held her in her arms. "There, there. It's all work out somehow, Azlea. It will all work."

Kevin Douglas Hazzard had his doubts. They still had a long way to go.

Chapter Twelve
The Pearl Kings

Jonathan Wells, Otto Van Dyke's Far Eastern manager, sat at the head of a small table, his nut-brown complexion and brown eyes troubled, tense. He was a small man, thin , had the bad color of one who had lived many years in the tropics. Sparse hair was plastered to his head with perspiration. Even through his look of worry, however, there was courage in his indomitable face, shrewdness to his canny straightforward eyes.

Jonathan Wells toyed with the pineapple drink before him, swished it about in the glass so the ice made musical tinklings. He looked at the other four men in the room. One of them was an elderly Chinese. His name was Kwoon. dressed in pongee silk, like the others, he was fat, wore tortoise-shelled glasses, boasted a Mandarin mustache with flowing ends.

Next to him sat a dapper Japanese, Hiko Yokida. Across the table was a Greek, August Papatonous. The last man was Ahmed, an Arab.

The five were seated in a private room of the Raffles Hotel, in Singapore. It was an ill-assorted group. Yet, at the least, these men represented millions of Straits dollars.

They were the pearl kings of the world.

Regardless of where a pearl was found, in the Indian Ocean, the Gulf of California, the Arabian Sea, a hundred and one little South Sea islands, it eventually passed through the hands of one of these five men before it reached a world market. Jonathan Wells, representing the fabulous Van Dyke interests, was at the head of the table.

"Ja Mynheers," Jonathan Wells said slowly, "this is certainly a bad business. The Singapore market is flooded with magnificent pearls. I have checked with Batavia, with Padang, even with Amsterdam. None of my agents is able to explain it. Yet," Wells shrugged nervously, "the pearls descend upon the markets. Already the price is down many Straits dollars here in Singapore. It is inexplicable."

"By Allah, we must find the reason!" thundered the Arab, pounding the table with his fist. "These pearls do not come from the Arabian Sea or the Gulf of Oman, my territories. But in Cairo, my brothers say by radio, the price of pearls is down twenty piasters per grain. It is ruinous!"

"Yess," the Japanese said hissingly. "It is the same in Tokyo. My firm will pay many yen to stop this illicit trafficking in these pearls. They are genuine pearls, as we all know. Perhaps some pearler has found some hidden cache ..."

Jonathan Wells shook his head. "It cannot be that, Mynheer. We all know that. No one bed of pearls, even if left unmolested since the Mogul emperors, could yield so huge a number of first water pearls. I am mystified."

August Papatonous, the swarthy Greek, leaned across the rattan table. His black eyes bored into those of Jonathan Wells. "Listen to me, Jonathan. Rumors tells us that Otto Van Dyke makes seed pearls by a secret new process. So far, we learn, these are very small and cheap pearls such as the Japanese have in their culture beds. Could it be possible that your firm" – a sneer creased his oily face – "has discovered a way to make big pearls?"

He sat back, pulled an Egyptian cigarette from a diamond-studded case, held the flame of an ornate lighter to its tip. The heavy smoke was like incense in the room.

Kwoon, the obese Chinese, leaned close to the Greek and tapped him on the arm. "Do not throw veiled hints as to the dishonesty of your colleagues or they may do likewise," he warned in a softly nasal voice.

He looked to the others. "My friend Van Dyke, peace to his ancestors, is beyond reproach, higher than these suspicious, unfounded rumors. We gain nothing by hurling accusations at each other. We must unite or lose the markets it has taken our firms generations to create, to weld together for the good of all."

Jonathan Wells nodded in accord, the worry lines imprinted in heavy crow's feet at the corners of his harried eyes. He had reason to be worried.

The pearl markets of the world were glutted with first water specimens. The five of them seated at this table, he knew, controlled the pearls of the world. They were doled out as not to fluctuate the market, were handled so that the demand always seemed to exceed the supply. Long years ago they had copied the DeBeers system.

In Africa, the DeBeers diamond mines produced just enough gems to cause no flurry in the market, to keep the stones steadily increasing in price each year. They were doing the same with pearls here in Singapore.

Only now, from some unknown source, hundreds of pearls were reaching the world markets at prices considerably under those offered by the syndicate. It was a damnable thing. Should it continue, it meant tremendous losses.

Jonathan Wells said: "I cabled our New York office the other day and our good friend, Jubal Beck, answered me this morning. He is distraught over the news. He says none of the pearls have apparently reached America yet, but he is worried. Mr. Beck is checking in San Francisco personally to see if he can find out anything. There's a bare chance he may take the Pan American Clipper and visit us for a short while here in Singapore."

Jonathan Wells had other worries, too. His employer, and dear friend, Otto Van Dyke, had landed in Singapore as if in a trance. He was ill of some strange malady, unable to talk coherently, to think. In his company was a man by the name of Nomar Samadi. Wells did not know him. But he recognized the power of attorney Samadi held and signed by Van Dyke.

Samadi was listed on that document as having full and complete charge of the vast Van Dyke organization. Already Jonathan Wells had been told in no uncertain terms that his employ with the company was to cease in sixty days.

Then too, the radio messages told Jonathan Wells that Rima, Van Dyke's only child, had been blown to bits in a laboratory explosion at a New York college. It all was so sudden, so discouraging after forty years spent with his employer. Jonathan Wells sighed.

He said, "I have further bad news, gentlemen. You have wondered why I am taking the place of Herr Van Dyke in this conference. The truth is" – pain made his eyes close for a second – "Otto Van Dyke is – dying!"

Incredulous surprise made the others silent. Wells continued. "His daughter and only heir was accidentally killed some weeks ago in New York. I do not yet know what will become of the firm – afterward."

He had received detailed instructions from Samadi not to divulge the new ownership of the Van Dyke interests. Wells wondered where Nomar Samadi could be. He had sent Van Dyke to the hospital upon their arrival in Singapore, then disappeared. Wells had tried to trace him but to no avail.

"But gentlemen," Jonathan Wells face now was gray with a worry that soured his insides, "that's is not all. I have learned what I tell you now, from my own sources." He lowered his voice, whispered : "I have learned that the Red Maggot has returned to the South Seas!"

Exclamations in four different tongues met Jonathan Wells' ears. He looked around the circle of paled faces, saw the same fear there he know lay mirrored in his own visage.

"By Allah!" swore Ahmed, "that means all nations save the Malays will have to go elsewhere for trade! It means..."

"Sabotage – perhaps war!" concluded the little Japanese, Yokida.

"But there is one gleam of sunshine," Jonathan Wells said slowly. "For some reason I have not heard from Paul Dupres, our technical expert on Van Dyke's Lost Island where we have our culture station. In the past he communicated with me by radio once weekly. Perhaps something is wrong with the sending apparatus, I do not know.

"But a Dutch vessel picked up a radio message from there a few hours ago, the first in several weeks. It was relayed to me by the wireless operator, a nephew of mine. It said"..." Jonathan Wells took a bit of paper from his pocket, read :

"Thomas Floyd's yacht now at island. With him is Captain Hazzard. Hazzard is leaving by plane after apparent receipt of news item. Proceed with plan as discussed with girl. Hazzard will see her adrift and go to her rescue. Once aboard, she will force his return to the island and Floyd's yacht now on route to Singapore. Hazzard is dangerous and must be kept under surveillance."

"Gentlemen," Jonathan Wells looked at the others, "something very menacing has happened. I am positive Paul Dupres did not send this message. Lost Island must be in the hands of pirates! It is my supposition that the parties responsible for returning the Red Maggot to the Maylay territory are now using Lost Island as their headquarters!"

"But who is this Captain Hazzard?" queried August Papatonous. "Is he a member of the American Military? And if so, what is his part in all this? I don't understand."

"Sometimes, dear August, your lack of knowledge in regards to world affairs is appalling," old Kwoon said, shaking his head. "The exploits of Captain Hazzard and his men are known around the world."

"Well I still have never heard of him," retorted the annoyed Greek. "So what exactly is it he does in these... ah... exploits of his?"

Jonathan Wells nodded to Kwoon. "Please, let me. Captain Kevin Douglas Hazzard is one of the most remarkable men in the whole world. He is an inventor, explorer, aviator, scientist and tireless warrior in the cause of justice. In America, the newspapers have christened him the Champion of Justice.

"He fights crime, Mynheers. When the safety or peace of his country is at stake, you will find Captain Hazzard and his team of loyal companions in the thick of things. And he always triumphs. I wonder," he mused, "if you realize what the return of the Red Maggot means to the United States? That country has no vast stake here as my fatherland, the British, the Japanese. But gentlemen, they have deep financial ties to Manila and the Philippines!"

Jonathan Wells nodded, touched a vesta to a slim Sumatra cheroot. "With unrest here, eventually the United States would lose Manila – the entire Philippine group – to our common enemy. We know that before long these natives would be banded together by unprincipled leaders, cause a war that might be the end of civilization. Mynheers, if Captain Hazzard is on our side, we have a chance – a bare chance."

Jonathan Wells looked at his watch. It was seven-thirty. He rang a bell on the table and a Malay waiter opened the door. Behind him, in the hallway were two others.

"You may serve the meal now," Wells told him. "We are somewhat in a hurry this evening."

With swift steps, the Malay waiter crossed the room and flashed a glance from the low-silled window. He recrossed toward the door, opened it, turned to Jonathan Wells.

"Saja tuan," he said bowing slightly. Wells frowned. The waiter was not the usual boy who served them whenever they met at the Raffles. It seemed strange. Jonathan Wells turned to the others at the table, but they were talking busily, paying no attention to the new waiter. Wells shrugged, took a puff on his cheroot. This entire Red Maggot affair was making him overly suspicious.

The Malaysian waiter at the door was handed a huge platter covered over with a silver cover such as used to keep foods hot while being served. He walked to a serving table against the wall and placed the huge platter in its center. The other two waiters followed, each with plates of salad. They kept their eyes down as they moved.

The last one entering the private room carefully closed the door, and only Jonathan Wells saw him deftly lock it. The slight Wells started to his feet, now convinced something was awry.

For, with the speed of striking cobras, the three waiters turned. Jonathan Wells got a flash of the platter under the raised silver cover. He gasped, eyes widening, for there was no food there. Only three revolvers fitted with silencers!

The waiter who had spoken to him, spat out, his black eyes venomous points of flame : "It is the end, you fools! The perils of the corrupt world are represented by you five foreign devils. Now you will pay for you crimes against our people! With your deaths we will control the pearl markets of the world! Accursed foreign dogs, prepare to die!"

He, and two companions, raised their silenced guns, their fingers straining on the triggers.

Suddenly, with a loud crash, the locked door was kicked opened, the latch breaking off. Captain Hazzard rushed into the room, his .45 automatic in his hand, spitting flames. The three assassins were caught flatfooted, as they tried in vain to turn and return fire. Hazzard's aim was uncanny, three loud shots and each of the would-be killers cried out and crumbled to the floor never having fired a single shot.

Captain Hazzard stood over them, kicked the revolvers away from their bodies. The leader was dead, a bullet through his throat, while the other two were severely wounded; one with a stomach wound, the other with a hole in his shoulder. Neither was a threat any longer, and lay moaning in pain at his feet.

Jonathan Wells was on his feet, face ashen. His right hand came into view, and in his fingers was a small Webley automatic. Hazzard looked at the man and his gun and grinned.

"You can put that away, Mr. Wells. You won't need it now."

Wells lowered his pistol and approached. As the color returned to his cheeks, he studied their timely savior and a light of recognition shone in his eyes.

"You must be... Captain Hazzard?"

Hazzard holstered his .45 and shook Wells' offered hand. "Yes, I am. And it seems I arrived in the nick of time."

"That you did, Captain. But how on earth did you know we were jeopardy?"

"While walking along the hallway, on my way here, I passed a janitors closet and heard someone making noise inside. When I opened the door, I found three naked men tied and gagged. As soon as I'd removed the gag from one of them, he explained how they'd been taken by these killers while on their way to serve you gentlemen dinner.

"I knew there was no time to call the authorities, so I came ahead and arrived outside just in time to hear one of these men harangue against you. Given a few more minutes, I might have been able to unlock the door, but I thought expediency was clearly the order of the day."

"A very wise decision on your part, Captain." Jonathan Wells indicated his associates, still seated at the table, like frozen statues. "We all owe you our lives."

Captain Hazzard merely nodded, his mind already on their next course of action. He pointed to the wounded men. "These men should be taken to a hospital immediately, Mr. Wells. I don't expect the authorities will ever make them talk, but we can keep them confined once their wounds are taken care of."

"I'll call the hotel manager," Wells said, "and tell him to notify the police and get an ambulance here. I still cannot believe these men were actually going to murder us."

"They are zealots," Hazzard clarified. "So filled with superstitious fervor of the return of the Red Maggot to the South Seas that they will kill or be killed in the cause of their beliefs."

He looked towards the broken door as he heard noise from the hallway followed by a half dozen excited voices. "It appears the freed waiters have already summoned the management."

The talk grew louder until several heads poked in and cautiously surveyed the room before entering. A tall man in a silk suit identified himself as the hotel's assistant manager. He was accompanied by a British police offer in khaki shorts, sporting a thick gray walrus mustache. He was introduced as Constable Weatherly. He took in the three bodies on the floor with the slightest raised eyebrow, then faced Jonathan Wells and Hazzard politely requesting an explanation.

In very concise sentences, Jonathan Wells told of the attack and Captain Hazzard's timely rescue. While the seasoned British copper was interviewing the other four pearl agents, Hazzard pulled Wells aside and whispered in his ears, "Say nothing of the Red Maggot."

In five minutes Constable Weatherly's men had supervised the clearing of the room of the dead and two wounded Malays. He then advised the pearl dealers that a guard would posted outside in the corridor. Eventually each would have to report to police headquarters to give their statements. The constable departed and Wells and his colleagues, all except Kwoon now on their feet, began to discuss their situation and what they could do to protect themselves in the future.

As they conferred, Captain Hazzard crossed to the open window, peered out. Suddenly he fell back, motioned the others away and held up his hand for silence.

The startled Mr. Yokida and Papatonous stepped away from the screened window. As they did so there was the quick swish of something flying through the air, the metallic tearing of the upper half of the screen. a streak of silvery light darted across the room, narrowly missing Jonathan Wells' neck. There was a sharp thud, then silence.

"Mien Gott, look!"

Jonathan Wells pointed with trembling forefinger at the wall behind them. The others turned, watched with incredulous eyes as Captain Hazzard strode to the wall, jerked a silver kris free from where it was embedded in the paneling!

"I thought so," he said matter-of-factly. "An old trick to strike fear into a group of people."

"It's working," Ahmed gasped still trying to catch his breath. "First those assassins and now this! I, for one, am petrified!"

"Look," said Wells, "there appears to be a note wrapped around it!"

Captain Hazzard's swift fingers unwound a length of jute which held a folded sheet of rice paper to the haft of the Malay kris. He read it, looked at the pearl merchants, a knowing smile on his face.

"I think," he began, "we will have to be very careful tonight. Our unknown enemy is determined to frighten us off. Too bad we can't let the British authorities know of the possibility of the Red Maggot returning to Singapore." He tapped the note in his hand, read aloud:

"Do not think that you have won even a small victory tonight. As the clock strikes midnight one of your number will die! Which one will it be? Only death will show you!"

As expected, the note was unsigned.

Jonathan Wells' somber voice said slowly, but vibrant with triumph: "I am not afraid – now!"

Chapter Thirteen
Sting of Doom

aptain Hazzard took immediate command of the situation. The assistant manager was called again and arrangements made to secure a large suite on the top floor of the hotel. As they walked towards the bank of elevators, Ahmed, the Arab, turned to the manager; a Mr. Wiley.

"Down below you will see a very devil of a man waiting for me in the lobby. His name is Ali Mohamid. Be so kind as to tell him to come up and join me in this room we are now going to. If I am going to die, I want him at my side, and we'll see how many of these accursed assassins go along with us to Paradise." His laugh was deep in his throat.

"Hold on," Captain Hazzard stepped up to the laughing Arab. "This Ali Mohamid, are you sure you can trust him?"

"Aie," Ahmed growled, looking offended. "Even though he is a convert to the true faith, I've known the rascal for many years and love him like the desert brother he is to me." His laugh boomed. "Many a man have we sent on that long journey together, Captain."

Hazzard nodded, as they exited the elevator. For now he would have to take Ahmed's word. He walked with the others to the safety of the luxury suite, closed and locked it. Shortly afterward there was a knock and Hazzard ushered Ali Mohamid in to join them. He was a big man, wore the clothes of western civilization awkwardly, forever tugging at his shirt collar and pulling on his tie. His left eye had been lost in some misadventure of the past, and a livid kris mark slanted across one cheek and dented the beak of his long nose. Hazzard was reminded of his own, nearly invisible scar that crossed over his left eye.

As Ahmed handed his friend a drink and introduced him to the group, Captain Hazzard drew Jonathan Wells aside, whispered the news that Otto Van Dyke was recovering. A subtle poison had been found in the old German's blood, introduced in some diabolically mysterious manner. It was Hazzard's vast knowledge of toxicology that first put hospital physicians on the right track.

Jonathan Wells was also told that Rima was alive. He was given a brief account of the happenings in New York, the fake article in the newspaper and the dash eastward in the Cora Marie. Hazzard told him of stopping at Lost Island, but did not tell of his underwater encounter with the deadly diver. He was not surprised when Wells did not mention a secret entrance to the island. It was Hazzard's belief that this secret passage must have been discovered by the plotters after taking control of the island.

"You say the yacht will dock tomorrow night?" Jonathan Wells asked.

"Yes," Captain Hazzard nodded. "The Cora Marie is headed for Singapore under forced draft, should reach here about dusk tomorrow or a little later."

"So, you believe this Samadi is the one behind these strange happenings? From what you say, it seems certain he is the one who stole the Red Maggot."

Wells face became grave. "That accursed pearl has caused men to go mad for the lust of power these thousands of years! It makes of the brain a cancerous growth. Should it reappear in the Malay States, it means perpetual unrest until it is destroyed. But it must be utterly done away with!"

He thought a moment and looked deeply into Hazzard's frosty blue-gray eyes, now almost black with intensity. "I am very relieved you are here, Captain. There is no other man I would trust in this situation," he said honestly and stretched out his hand.

There was another knock at the door. "Who is it?" Captain Hazzard asked, preparing to unlock the latch."

"It's me, Captain," replied the voice of Tyler Randall.

The blonde giant walked past the captain, who relocked the door immediately. "Looks like you've been stirring up a hornet's nest around here," he grinned. "There are tons of reporters wanting to know about some shooting earlier and all kinds of British cops on the street outside."

"I'll explain later," Captain Hazzard said. "Right now tell me what you've learned?"

A frown masked Tyler's face. "Bad news, sir. I allowed Azlea to escape as you ordered. I thought I wouldn't have any trouble following her, as was your plan. But she's a tricky one, Captain. She wove in and out of these little harbor alleys and she lost me. I'm really sorry, Captain. I let you down."

Captain Hazzard slapped his pilot's arm. "Don't apologize. No real harm has been done, Randall. The girl is only a tool of the man responsible for all this : Nomar Samadi. Perhaps this will cause him to become careless, step out into the open."

After this exchange, Hazzard related all that had transpired since his fortuitous arrival and subsequent shoot-out with the three bogus waiters.

He was ending his monologue just as Jonathan Wells came over and introductions were made. Wells looked up at Tyler, his yellow hair and smiled, "If you don't have some Viking blood in you, Mr. Tyler, then I'm not a true son of the fatherland."

"Your heritage is safe, Mr. Wells. My grandparents came from Norway and settled in Nebraska where they became wheat farmers."

As fascinating as Tyler Randall's family history was, Hazzard politely turned the conversation to the situation at hand. "Rima is still at the hospital with her father?" he inquired.

"Yes, sir. Mr. Van Dyke is coming along nicely now, after you helped them diagnose the poison. He's still unconscious and they say it will be a few more days before he comes around."

Captain Hazzard absentmindedly tug at the corner of his mustache, worry creasing his brow. "I am worried about Paul Dupres, Mr. Wells. It is my guess he is on Lost Island, a prisoner of Samadi's gang. I understand from Miss Van Dyke this Dupres is a brilliant technician. Should he meet his death it would be a terrible crime. And – I mean to prevent it! We must return to the island as quickly as possible and attempt a rescue – if it isn't too late."

Jonathan Wells wholeheartedly agreed. He told them of the radio message from the island picked up by his nephew on the Dutch tramp.

"It ties up with what you've told me, Captain. Lost Island is in the hands of this Samadi and his men. Dupres is absolutely trustworthy. If this Eurasian girl attempted to trap him, I fear Dupres is dead. We must be very careful in any action we attempt. Samadi drugged my employer, forced him to sign the power of attorney. And now he has vanished."

"Yes," Captain Hazzard said. "The motive behind this plot becomes clear now. The maggots of lust have entered the soul of Nomar Samadi. With the Red Maggot, and the Van Dyke process for making perfect pearls, he will be able to raise millions of dollars, control the superstitious natives, endeavor to make the South Seas a place only for the Dyaks, the Malays and the wild bushmen of the interior."

"But Captain," Tyler Randall seemed confused and scratched his head. "It is their home. Why shouldn't they have control of it? Is that so bad?"

"No, Randall, sovereignty should ultimately belong to the people of these countries. But not as they are now, illiterate, savage cannibals living one step above animals in their jungle domains."

"Not all foreign interests are here to exploit the natives," Jonathan Wells picked up Hazzard's side. "Countries like America, Germany and others want to help bring the Dyaks and the Malays into the twentieth century. To provide them with a better, civilized way of life, now and for future generations to come.

"Noble goals, Mr. Randall, that will all be for naught if Samadi and his type take over the South Seas. They have no desire to see the natives prosper, but would rather keep them locked in the dark ages of ignorance and brutality. They must not be allowed to succeed!"

It was a lot for Tyler Randall to digest. Still, he was happy to know his boss was as ever on the side of truth and justice.

There was a sudden sharp knock at the door. Captain Hazzard opened it, stepped back in astonishment as a slight, determined figure stepped into the room. It was Jubal Beck.

Beck's jaw went slack with surprise as he recognized Hazzard and he began to stammer. "Why... wha... what are you doing here, Captain Hazzard?" he cried. They shook hands, then the jeweler greeted Jonathan Wells and the others whom he had evidently met before.

Beck then looked at Hazzard, rubbed his chin with his forefinger. "Let me guess. You're still trying to say that accursed Red Maggot is stolen, is back here in the South Seas," he said.

"It is here in the South Seas, Beck," Hazzard said clearly. "I know because I was with Miss Van Dyke when she opened the safe later that same night of the strange accidents. I..."

"Miss Rima – the Red Maggot!" Beck exclaimed. Then : "The girl – you mean she is alive! The Maggot stolen! I – I thought it was all imaginative, a – a sort of melodramatic story your newspaper associate, Crawley, was concocting for a feature story."

Captain Hazzard related what had happened after he and Thomas Floyd had left the Van Dyke store that cold night in New York.

"That explains something else, then," Jubal Beck said reflectively, forefinger rubbing his pointed chin. "Two days later I changed the recording paper in the door lock of the shop and noted it had been opened much later that night of the accidents. I thought the lock was simply recording incorrectly, had it changed. So, Miss Rima is alive, you say. What wonderful news. But how is Mr. Van Dyke? I've just landed from a plane an hour ago and have not been to the hospital yet."

He sighed, shook his head. "If I only knew what this is all about! I received a cryptic cable from that fellow, Nomar Samadi, saying he had taken over the Van Dyke interests. It was the customer who was in the store when the tar vat exploded. You remember, I described him to you that night."

"Yes," Hazzard said. "Continue. What else did his message say?"

"He... he says I will not be needed after the first of the month, and..." Beck's face was ashen.

"I understand," Hazzard spoke quietly, "you were attacked by gunmen that same night. I read of it in Crawley's story in the newspaper as we traveled to the West Coast. With Thomas Floyd's approval, I, and several of my men, accompanied him on his voyage."

Beck became excited. "Yes, and narrowly escaped death! Mr.

Wells cabled me. That's why I am here, Captain, I believe there's something to this affair that's far deadlier than the mere taking of the Red Maggot. Look," he held up his hand, counted off the fingers as he spoke.

"The attempt at Miss Rima, then my own escape. That makes two. I just landed, but already have heard Mr. Van Dyke was poisoned, that you saved his life. Probably, Captain Hazzard, attempts have also been made against you?" His greenish eyes were wide.

Hazzard's chuckle was low. In clipped sentences, he informed them of the airplane attack on the Cora Marie and went over the events of his brief stop at the island – without mentioning the encounter with the mysterious diver – the flight in the SeaBee and the finding of Azlea. Then he told of the attack by the waiters, the threat.

Jubal Beck suddenly was nervous. He looked at his watch. "Why, it – it's ten minutes of midnight now! All of us may be killed! They – this murderous killer – may start with – with me!"

Oval face pale, Beck looked at the others. Jonathan Wells walked over to the little man, encouraged him. But Beck was distraught and wouldn't be consoled. His face was streaming with perspiration.

"I – I had to come all the way to Singapore to – to be killed!" he moaned. "I thought I might help poor Mr. Van Dyke, and – and – now..." He was unable to finish the sentence.

Ahmed had no problems speaking. "By Allah, if I die it will be fighting!" he growled. From the waistband of his trousers he withdrew a long, curved knife. Jubal Beck stared at it in morbid fascination.

There was an eerie silence in the spacious room. On the desk a small electric clock made no noise, but its second hand seemed to race around the dial. The minute pointer was but one space from midnight.

Captain Hazzard, stoic in the background, heard Beck's strained breathing. The little Japanese merchant sat looking at his fingernails in utter disregard of all danger. The Greek, Papatonous, was sweating profusely. Kwoon sat blandly staring off into space. Jonathan Wells and Tyler Randall were immobile were they stood.

And then, at sixty seconds of midnight, something strange came to Hazzard's sensitive nostrils. He could not immediately place the strong odor. It was musky, faintly sickening, smelled unclean. Captain Hazzard's every nerve was tense now, his entire being watchful, vigilant.

And then the telephone on the desk rang.

Jubal Beck jumped off his seat, sucking in his breath in a strangled sob.

The Greek was also on his feet in a sudden start of terror. The others merely looked at the ringing telephone. From blocks away came a metallic bong, then another.

It was midnight.

Cautiously, showing no emotion, Captain Hazzard picked up the receiver from its cradle. He put the instrument to his ear, said: "Yes?"

"Ah, it's Captain Hazzard!" the voice over the telephone was oddly flat, devoid of inflection. "My dear Captain, the clock now is striking the appointed hour. As its last stroke sounds, one of you will perish – horribly. Perhaps it won't be you – this time! But later, Captain Hazzard, all of you will feel the bite of death!" There was a soft click as the line went dead.

Again, stronger now, came the odor of musk to Captain Hazzard's nostrils. He looked at the men assembled before him. They knew the phone call was from the one heading the gang of killers. But they didn't know which one was to die...

The slight scar over Hazzard's left eye seemed to flare, becoming a visible pink line. Randall had seen this effect whenever his leader was about to go into action.

"Ten – eleven..."

It was Kwoon, who was counting the strokes of the clock. They were a death knell in the hot night air.

"Twelve!"

And then, in a flash of understanding, the faint warnings in Hazzard's subconscious became acute. Across the room he saw Ahmed's man, Ali Mohamid, take a white handkerchief from his coat pocket, start to raise it to his streaming face.

And then the musky odor became as a blow in the face, so pungent was its scent. It suggested unspeakable horror, a deadly and menacing something of mystery. Captain Hazzard moved forward, the scar livid on his face, eyes blazing like twin beacons.

Then the incredible occurred. Hazzard, his senses warning him, leaped forward. But he was too late! Something horribly black and writhing was in Mohamid's silk handkerchief. The man, his face suddenly a mask of fury, drew back his arm and threw the black thing straight at Jonathan Wells' face!

Jubal Beck screamed, and was echoed by Papatonous' hoarse cry. Captain Hazzard made no sound. His face grim, without fear. Like a bolt of lightning, far quicker than the stabbing strike of a rattlesnake, Hazzard's hand, opened flat, darted out at the arcing deadly squirming thing in mid-air. His hard palm slapped the thing aside where it fell to the floor.

Almost in the same motion, Hazzard's left came around, the granite knuckles made a sound like the blast of a revolver on Mohamid's brown chin. The man's eyes rolled upward. He sucked in a breath, fell headlong across the rug. His lax, nerveless hand fell inches from the dazed creature on the floor.

The swift black creature moved in on long, hideously hairy legs. It hurled its loathsome shape at the unprotected hand. A black tail curled over its glistening back and stabbed once, then again. The fearsome black scorpion would have struck a third time had not Tyler Randall rushed forward and stomped on it with this boot, a look of mixed horror and disgust on his face.

"The deadly black scorpion!" Captain Hazzard said tautly. "It shows the lengths this Samadi will go to in order to win his objective. He must have bribed Ahmed's man with a very large sum of money to do this, after his own attempt with the waiters failed. As you know, the black scorpion is utterly fearless, will attack the first thing it sees. I thought I smelled its musky odor but wasn't certain. You see, the scorpion had been partially anesthetized, I presume, given just enough to last until the stroke of midnight."

"Is he dead?" Jonathan Wells asked Tyler Randall, now kneeling beside the motionless Mohamid. He felt for a pulse and failed to find one. {7}

"Yes," Randall said, dropping the lifeless hand and rising.

Ahmed came over and bending over, spit in the dead man's face.

{7 **AUTHOR'S NOTE:** Ordinarily speaking, a scorpion's sting it not necessarily fatal to a man. Yet many cases have come to the writer's attention of fatal results after being stung by the large black scorpion. Black scorpions 8 inches long in width are not uncommon. A number of deaths have been noted in the public press due to the bite of the Black Widow spider, many times smaller than an 8 inch black scorpion; therefore death is not improbable should one be stung by a scorpion of this size.}

"His hard palm slapped the thing aside..."

"Son of a desert jackal!" Anger raged within him. "May your worthless soul rot in hell through eternity!"

"Go easy, fellah," the pilot advised. "This isn't going to do any good."

Ahmed glared at the tall Yank. "He was not your friend."

Captain Hazzard quickly took charge again. "It's obvious Mohamid had instructions to throw the scorpion into Wells' face. Samadi wants first to kill of all those in the Van Dyke concern. That way no one could dispute his claims to the Van Dyke business, he would be safe. I don't believe there will be any more attacks tonight gentlemen. I, for one, am ready for sleep. But," and Hazzard's face became set again, thoughtful, "I am positive Samadi will strike again tomorrow night!"

Chapter Fourteen
The Man Without a Face

On the outskirts of Singapore, on the hill overlooking the Kalang Reservoir, was a magnificent estate. It long had been known as a place of mystery, was unvisited by any person save in the dead of the tropic night. Stationed at the gateway of the outer grounds were two dacoits. These men originally came from India, but there are many Hindus in and around the Malay States.

These two dacoits – and others hidden from view by the screening shrubbery of flaming hibiscus, coconut palms and banana trees – were devotees of Thugee, the terrible practice of killing indiscriminately to placate some pagan god. Within the ground, fierce dholes roamed. The dholes, huge wild dogs known to pack together like wolves and hunt down tigers, also were imported from India.

Should any man chance to escape the vigilance of the guardians of the gate the wild dogs would stalk him down, tear him to bits. It was an impregnable stronghold, one calculated to keep the mind of the dweller within the boundaries completely at ease.

Nomar Samadi, his white teeth hidden behind rather tight lips, sat alone in an immense room of this house. He was ill at ease for he knew the man from whom he took his orders had cause to be angry with him. Nomar Samadi had never seen his master in this nefarious work.

Several months before he had been approached by a Malay he

had known for many years. In fact, they had been in prison together in Batavia. This Malay was the contact man for someone higher up, perhaps the head of the criminal organization.

Nomar Samadi's reputation always seemed to speed ahead of him. He was a murderer with a price on his head in Sumatra; an embezzler sought by the French in Cochin-China; and another murder charge was on him in Manila. Half the nations having mandated islands of the South Seas would give considerable amounts of money to lay their clutches upon the person of Nomar Samadi.

Strangely enough, he was practically unknown in Singapore. The knowledge of how thoroughly the British punish offenders had kept him away from the island. But this Malay pal had assured him he would be safe in Singapore, hence his secret entry into the city weeks before.

The game, Samadi recognized at once, was for high stakes. It meant a great deal of money, a trip to New York where he was quite safe, for he had never been to America. He had made that trip. But, and Samadi's dark face showed lines of worry about his black eyes, it had been unsuccessful in the main.

He had managed to steal a huge pearl called the Red Maggot, of which he had heard vague whisperings in the past, but other things had gone wrong. As they said in that strange city of New York, everything had gone "haywire."

A slight noise from across the expansive room made Samadi start. He peered in that direction, but saw nothing save an ornate Chinese screen embroidered in reds, greens and gold with the figures of two flying dragons. Red fire shot from their open mouths and underneath was a paddy field devastated by the searing flame.

Somehow it struck a responsive chord in Samadi's brain. For some reason that tugged at his subconscious, he was certain he didn't like that picture at all. It was so suggestive of the threats his mysterious boss made when he – Samadi – agreed to murder.

Again the slight noise came from behind the screen. It was very like the sound of the legs of a chair scraping gently against polished wood. Then, and Samadi felt squeamish, a grotesque shadow appeared on the screen. Samadi's teeth showed like bleached bones for a moment as his tongue moistened dry lips. There was a man seated behind the dragon screen!

And then Samadi almost cried aloud. For a voice, a thin, reedy and menacing voice, issued from behind the screen.

"It is well, Samadi," the voice said without inflection, "that you should contemplate your many errors of the past. People who make errors do not work for me – long! You have made many mistakes, Nomar Samadi, and now it is time to take stock of yourself so that more do not occur.

"Last night, in the Raffles Hotel, three of your men failed miserably when they had the pearl tycoons of the world closeted in a small dining room from which there was no escape. Later, the man you bribed, Ali Mohamid, bungled when he threw the black scorpion at the Jonathan Wells. You have..."

"It was that devil Captain Hazzard who caused it all," Samadi said quickly, and there was strain in his husky voice. "Everywhere I turn, his clever counter-attacks oppose me, defeat my most careful plans."

"Perhaps my judgment was wrong in thinking you were able to meet fire with fire, fight steel with steel." A regretful sigh came from the man behind the screen. "It would be too bad – for you – should I believe my judgment so greatly misplaced! But again, Samadi...

"Twice in New York your bungling men allowed Rima Van Dyke to escape: once at the chemical laboratory and again after she escaped. Then I was fooled for a number of days, as were you, by the fake news item of her death which appeared in the papers. It..."

"Hazzard again!" Samadi interrupted fiercely. "He was responsible for everything, I tell you. Somehow he managed to defeat the bombing attack I ordered on Thomas Floyd's yacht as they were leaving coast of California. The plane never returned. I tell you Hazzard isn't human!"

"You will allow me to finish," the voice snapped coldly and then resumed. "At Long Island it must have been you also who authorized the diver to attack Captain Hazzard underwater when he went down in Thomas Floyd's diving ball. That was a particularly stupid mistake, Samadi, for it told this do-gooder adventurer that Lost Island was in the hands of Van Dyke's enemies."

"It would not have seemed stupid if our diver had succeeded in killing Hazzard!" Samadi almost came out of his chair.

"But he did not succeed!" barked the angry voice. "Once again you failed miserably. And then, adding stupidity upon stupidity, you sent a radio message to the tramp steamer telling them to try and trap Captain Hazzard as he flew to Singapore. Any number of ships might have accidentally intercepted that message.

"But before that you got panicky, radioed me in code here in Singapore to get Hazzard away from the island as quickly as possible. It necessitated my agent in the hospital increasing the dosage of poison he was giving Van Dyke so his approaching death would be sent out on the radio broadcast. I fear now that was an unnecessary risk to take. Van Dyke was so completely in our power with the drug you had administered on the Pacific Clipper there was no need to panic. Rather we might have killed him for nothing.

"Speaking of which, does that fool, Dupres, still refuse to serve as our technician in making the pearls on the island?"

"Y-yes, sir," Samadi replied. "Our man, LaGrange, says he doesn't need Dupres' assistance. I think though …" and Samadi's red lips curled wolfishly away from his white teeth – "Dupres will change his mind before another week is past. He is in the vat of sea water, and the Coral Death is creeping up on him!"

"Splendid!" There was a note of sadistic triumph from the man behind the screen.

Nomar Samadi wished it were possible to see this man with whom he talked. But the screen hid everything save the grotesque shadow. He was talking to a man without a face.

Suddenly the man without a face clapped his hands together and Samadi saw a second shadow appear on the Chinese screen. Then he heard the voice utter a sharp command.

"Bring Azlea to me!"

There was quiet for nearly a minute. Then Samadi heard a slight shuffle behind him. He jerked his head around, gave a sharp sigh of relieve when he saw it was the Eurasian girl, Azlea. In her arms she held a small langur – East Indian monkey – and the intelligent creature had one arm about the girl's ivory neck. Samadi's eyes brightened a bit, roved boldly over her shapely figure. He liked this girl, and later, perhaps…

"Be seated, Azlea," the man behind the screen ordered curtly. He waited until Azlea took the chair next to that of Samadi's. In doing so, the slit along her green satin dress opened to reveal her well formed legs, which she crossed demurely at the ankles. Still, Samadi's eyes continued to drink in her blossoming sensuality.

"Twice you have failed, Azlea," the faceless voice accused. "You allowed this Captain Hazzard to throw you off balance by the sudden diving of his plane after missing him with your automatic at point blank aim.

"Then, during the time of the forced landing on the Barito, in Borneo, you were silly enough to almost jump into the mouth of a crocodile. During the confusion this man not only saved your life but also used the opportunity to fool the river Dyaks into thinking he was a god.

"Then," the voice continued with biting acidity, "you do not stay with his party when you had the chance. You steal away and return here. It would have been very easy for a woman of your – shall we say considerable charms? – to fool him, stimulate contriteness and thus better serve me – and yourself."

"But," she faltered, "you do not know this Captain Hazzard. Yes, you have all the facts, exactly as I reported them. But cold facts do not properly convey the essence of this remarkable man. He – he can do anything – do you hear me, anything! And as for my so-called charms, all the while he – he paid absolutely no attention to me. Rather he had that the white girl, Rima Van Dyke…"

"My dear Azlea, surely one of your rare beauty, and wiles, need fear no woman," the voice from behind the screen said softly. He sighed. "I fear this Captain Hazzard must be in love with the Van Dyke girl…"

"NO!" Azlea was on her feet, face strained and little fists in clenched knots. "No, I tell you!" She was panting now with terrible anger. "I – will kill her, will…"

Samadi watched the Eurasian girl's overreaction with interest. It was obvious to him, and the faceless leader, that Azlea O'Hara was very jealous of Rima Van Dyke. There could be only one reason for such emotion, she had been swayed by the American hero. Samadi listened quietly, watching as his master manipulated the girl's feelings to his own advantages.

"But," the voice taunted softly, "I have reason to know he does love her, that he despises you! It isn't the girl's fault, Azlea. It's the fault of Captain Hazzard. Do you think if I were in your place I would allow him to flaunt my love? No! I believe I would teach him what love meant by giving him my hatred – and six inches of steel in his heart.!"

"Yes!" Azlea panted furiously. "I hate him! I will do as you say. I will kill him! Oh, please, give me this last chance! I swear to you he will die before the night is over. I swear it!"

Chapter Fifteen
Ambush on the Docks

"I have a plan that may help you achieve that end, my dear Azlea," the voice from behind the screen said cunningly. "But first, Samadi, I'll have to admit you did two good jobs in capturing Jonathan Wells and Van Dyke for me. Wells is below now. I shall get to him after a while. It was clever the way you got Otto Van Dyke away from the hospital as well. You sent him to Lost Island by plane immediately. Correct?"

"Yes," Samadi nodded, taking heart from these words of approval. "I slipped him out about an hour ago. His daughter had just left him for the night, and won't be checking up until her return in the morning. It was all rather simple. My men told the hospital doctors the girl had changed her mind and now that her father was recovering, although still unable to talk, she wanted him with her. The fools fell for it without asking for even the slightest bit of verification. Where it was so late, they never thought to call the Van Dyke girl at her hotel. Everything went as you planned, master."

Samadi laughed, curled the lips away from his white teeth. Azlea glanced at him, tried to restrain the shudder of dread that trembled through her body. The man reminded her of a giant, brown bug.

"That is fine, Samadi," their employer said. "Now we have a hold over the girl, can talk terms with her, force her to turn over her interests. But back to my plan to capture Captain Hazzard. Within the next two hours Thomas Floyd's yacht will dock at the Old Wharf. As you know, the British fleet has just finished maneuvers and occupy all but those old, native docks.

"Where the Cora Marie will berth is nearly deserted. The few craft there are native boats, a few Chinese junks and Indian dhows. Hazzard will undoubtedly go to meet the ship when she docks. He'll most likely go down to the area in a rickshaw, probably take his companion and the Van Dyke girl with him. Perhaps he may even take Jubal Beck, the New York manager, along with him. Thus he will step into my trap.

"The second he steps foot on those ancient docks, he will be surrounded by my lascars and dacoits, will be allowed to make a run for it, and his party will be hemmed in so that the only safety that offers itself will be aboard a particular old dhow!

"No one knows I have installed silenced motors in this dhow and you can put to sea in order to get rid of the bodies, once they have been dealt with permanently." The man without a face laughed and it had a reedy, eerie pitch that sent little prickles up and down Samadi's back.

"There, Samadi, on the dhow, you and Azlea will form a reception committee of two..." the voice became thick with menace and the promise of a terrible retaliation – "you know what to do! Captain Hazzard, all who are with him, must die tonight!"

Azlea O'Hara was on her feet, her almond eyes half-closed with evil purpose. Her breasts rose and fell under the stress of her emotion as she said, voice as brittle as ice dropping on glass : "I promise that Captain Hazzard will die tonight!"

Azlea hurried from the main room, followed by the grinning Samadi. He caught up with her in the hall and grabbed hold of her arm.

"A word with you, Miss O'Hara," he pleaded, his oily words falling from his lips. She glared at the hand on her elbow and he let go. "There is no need for us to strangers. After all, we are working together for our master."

"What is it you are trying to say?" the girl said bluntly. She detested dealing with the brown skinned rogue. "Spit it out, man!"

"I can be good for you, Azlea," he took a bold step nearer, his hand reaching up to her face. "One of such beauty should be put on a pedestal and adored. Given beautiful baubles. I can do that," a leer clouded his beady eyes, "and much more, if you would be... ah... think of me in the same way you once did of Captain Hazzard."

Azlea heard this word and her mind recoiled, as her head did from the reaching fingers. Suddenly she lashed out and slapped Samadi's face, rocking him back on his heels in painful shock.

"Keep your hands off me, you diseased son of a pig!" She backed away from him, her free hand waving in the air. "We may have to work together, but that is all there will ever be between us. Suggest anything more, ever again, and I swear I will scratch out your eyes and feed them to my monkey!" With that she hurried off, holding the furry pet so tightly that it whimpered in pain.

For a second, Nomar Samadi stood like a statue, his hand touching his bruised cheek where the girl's hand had struck. Then an awful red fury filled his being, as the indignity of her attack sank in. Damn the hussy and her self-inflated image. Who did she think she was? Some kind of lady? She was nothing but a half-breed native who needed to be shown her proper place in the scheme of things. And he would be the one to show her! When this assignment was finished and the leader had no further use of Miss Azlea O'Hara, Nomar Samadi would claim her; and she would capitulate or she would suffer the consequences. Then his dark imagination began to think such punishment might be even more satisfying.

But all that was for later, now he must follow his orders. He knew what he must do. This night he would make Captain Hazzard pay for his victories. Pay not only with Hazzard's death but with agony that was worse than death...

Samadi laughed aloud in anticipation for the night's work and exited the lonely mansion on a hill.

The man behind the Chinese screen smiled softly to himself as he heard his two minions quit the room. His fingers went to a sling arrangement under his arm, and when it came into view a magnificent red pearl was in the hollow of his hand.

It was the Red Maggot. The man caught his breath with the sheer beauty of it. But it was a malignant beauty. It emanated evil in its blood-red rays, took the very soul of the man staring at it and twisted, turned it into that of a skulking beast.

Wild thoughts of conquest permeated the man's brain, warped and deadened it to all human sensibilities. The Red Maggot was truly a gnawing and consuming living entity within the brain of the man who held it.

He got to his feet, his face a mask of sadistic cunning. Beneath the floor on which he stood were the cellars, and there, confined in a small cubicle of concrete was Jonathan Wells. The man slipped the Red Maggot into the pouch, walked eagerly towards the entrance of the stairs which led below...

The short dusk of the tropic nightfall was setting in. Captain Hazzard, Rima Van Dyke and Tyler Randall stood at the curb in front of the Raffles Hotel. Hazzard held up his hand, and three rickshaws stepped from line and advanced, putting their shafts to the street so the three could climb within.

"The Old Wharf," Hazzard directed in Chinese, for the three rickshaw men were of that country. In a moment, the three rickshaws abreast, they were proceeding at a leisurely pace toward the Old Wharf.

Captain Hazzard was eager to sit down with Thomas Floyd and learn what had transpired aboard the Cora Marie, after he and the others had flown off. Of course he was also anxious to see how the cowboy, Jake Cole, was holding up in his new role as a South Seas sailor. He could already imagine the string of cuss words that would emerge from the wrangler's mouth when they finally docked. Of course Jake would be very upset that he had missed out on all the action in Borneo and here in Singapore.

As they moved along the crowed island streets, Captain Hazzard had no way of knowing the three Chinese rickshaw "boys" were Samadi's men. But, deep within his exceptional mind, with its heightened sixth sense, a precognitive stab of warning caused him to become restless, preoccupied.

Captain Hazzard did not verbally communicate with his companions regarding his feelings, but he did send his pilot a silent, telepathic alert. Randall, be wary! I am sensing danger ahead. Stay sharp, say nothing to the girl!

Tyler Randall caught Hazzard's eye and gave him a very small nod with his head, silently acknowledging his receipt of the warning. Captain Hazzard had no personal fear, but he did feel responsible for the safety of those accompanying him. He could depend on Randall in a fight, but now he wished the girl had stayed at the hotel. With Nomar Samadi still on the loose, he should have thought twice before inviting her along. Rima Van Dyke had had more than her share of harrowing experiences these past forty-eight hours.

But her father, now safe in the hospital, was in a deep normal sleep, probably would awaken in the morning with no memory of his capture by Samadi and the long journey from New York.

Captain Hazzard looked about him. They were approaching the Old Wharf now, had left Occidental invention and improvement behind them, as if slipping into the past. Here only native craft tied up. There were Chinese junks, sampans with lateen sails furled, huge dhows from India, a rusty tramp or two. Here were the sights and smells of the true Far East; the sourness of bilge, the stench of fish and all intermingled with the heady odor of spices, the penetrating aroma of green coffee.

Occasionally a furtive figure of a Dyak showed momentarily in the gathering dusk. The native would watch them with no sign of friendliness. And, several times, the Dyak would slip after the three rickshaws with stealthy feet, keeping out of sight in the shadows cast by the godowns, or warehouses.

To keep up the pretense that nothing was wrong, Randall had engaged Rima in an animated conversation about Chinese cuisine. The girl wondered why Captain Hazzard remained silent, almost morose.

Suddenly Hazzard held up his hand. With a low command he ordered the three rickshaw boys to halt. They did so, and to Rima's astonishment, vanished into the surrounding shadows. Hazzard stepped to the rotted boards of the wharf, motioned to the others to follow.

From around them came a soft pat-pat-pat of sound. Captain Hazzard frowned, wondered what it could be. And then, in a sudden flash of understanding, he recognized the macabre sound.

It was the patter of bare feet on the wharf! They were methodically being surrounded by Samadi's dacoits, his thugs and lascars!

"Look out!" he called out as a half dozen small, pajama clad Dyaks and Chinese rushed at them from all sides. Some were wielding wooden belaying pins, while others held knives and hatchets. Like a pack of starving hyenas falling on a wounded prey, the wild eyed butchers attacked.

Needing no second warning, Tyler Randall plowed his fist into the first man to reach him, lifting the fellow off his feet and sending him careering backwards into his mates. A second whipped a wicked hatchet at the tall blonde's head and he barely jerked it back in time to avoid being decapitated. Rima screamed, her knuckled fist covering her mouth, eyes wide in sheer terror.

Captain Hazzard stepped in front of her at the same time unleashing a series of swift punches and kicks at the oncoming fighters. They went down like candle-pins, one after another. "Stay between us!" He told the girl, positioning her in the middle of the battling pilot and himself.

Meanwhile the Viking blood in Randall's veins was asserting itself as he went into a battling frenzy. Tired of repeatedly dealing with one attacker at a time, bodily picked up his latest victim and hoisted him up over his head, heaved him high into the air to land atop the next wave of Samadi's forces.

"Come on!" he bellowed, reaching out to grab another screeching dacoit and hurl him into bloodthirsty mob. "Come and get it!"

"It's no good," Captain Hazzard quickly assessed their chances of survival. "There are too many of them, out here in the open!"

"So, what do we do?" the berserker-mad pilot asked, his voice near breathless from his efforts to keep warding off their attackers.

Images rolled through Hazzard's mind, particularly of their current surroundings until one stood out clearly. "Wait. I remember seeing an old Indian dhow up the wharf just a hundred yards or so. The gangplank was down. If we can make it there, perhaps there's a chance we can hold them at bay."

Randall drove his right fist into the tiny nose of a very unlucky dacoit. "Alright, Captain. I'm with you."

Captain Hazzard pulled out his .45 automatic and drilled two thugs, which instantly stopped the others in their tracks. He reached behind his back and grabbed Rima's hand. "Follow me, Randall. Our only chance is to make that dhow before they regroup!" He began pulling the girl with him as he started running. "Perhaps there's a boat we can launch, row back toward town. We can hold them off if we get on that water!"

No sooner were they running for all they were worth then a crazy yell rose up from the maddened throng and they gave chase, blood in their eyes.

Chapter Sixteen
The Cobra Death

Running quickly, but carefully through the pungent darkness, Captain Hazzard led the girl and Randall toward the old dhow which loomed ahead of them. Once again the champion of justice found himself comfortable in a stygian setting, able to discern shapes and objects and avoid them easily.

All those years as a blind youth had provided him with the uncanny ability to navigate near pitch black environment as this one.

Rima Van Dyke held on to his hand tightly, afraid to get lost should they become separated. Behind her he could feel Tyler Randall's towering presence as he guarded their rear. Within the first few steps of their flight, the pilot had pulled out his own automatic pistol.

A sudden gust of air hot as from a furnace swirled around them followed by an eerie clanking and creaking of lateen sails, the soft slap-slap of wavelets against the piling. It whimpered around masts that stuck up like dead fingers. A rat scampered almost from under their feet, squealed once and was gone.

The pat-pat-pat of feet seemed to be all around them. Dimly ahead a lone light glowed dismally, was so weak as to make no shadow. From afar came the slow ringing of a ship's bell. From miles away in the harbor a whistle sounded like a voice from some grisly sepulcher. No moon was overhead. It was as if the night were holding its breath, sitting back and silently witnessing the play of death before it.

The three reached the stern of the old dhow. It was motionless, but a faint creaking reached their ears. It was as if ghosts of a hundred years leered down at them, the ghosts of men murdered on a dozen seas and oceans, in strange, far away ports.

Now, stronger than ever, the warning of impending danger surged through Captain Hazzard's mind. But there could be no turning back now. The gangplank of the dhow was a few feet away. It swayed under their weight, threatened to capsize and plunge them into the foul water. Hazzard reached the top of the gangplank, stepped upon the seamed deck.

Then from the shadowy figures below on the dock arose a hissing sigh. Captain Hazzard tensed for it seemed more like a murmur of relief then one of disappointment. And then the terrible truth of their predicament impacted on his brain, momentarily stunned him. They were supposed to have taken refuge on the dhow!

Hazzard had led them into a cleverly laid death trap!

The old ship was as silent as the grave. No sound could be heard except an occasional, age-old creak of the teak with which it was constructed. From one of the pouches on his belt , Hazzard took out a small, heavy oblong piece of metal.

On the side of it was a tiny crank that folded down into the oblong box itself. He turned this crank perhaps twenty-times. From within came the slight whir of cogs, a thin, almost soundless noise as if some miniature flywheel was spinning at a tremendous rate.

It was a pocket flashlight and the turning of the crank caused a miniscule dynamo to generate electricity. A portion of the case folded back and uncovered a powerful light bulb. Captain Hazzard pressed a button and a brilliant beam of light knifed the deck of the old ship.

Rima Van Dyke almost cried aloud in startled surprise. Randall caught her arm, drew her close to him. Hazzard threw a quick glance toward the dock. He felt, rather than saw, the massed brown bodies there, the fierce faces upturned. Escape from them was impossible by way of the wharf.

He turned back again. And then the ghostly craft became alive. Not with figures, with anything that could be seen, but with menacing and grim rustlings and eerie creakings. It was as if a company of phantoms had climbed the hull, took position on the high poop deck, descended rigging, emerged from the hold to ring them in a circle of death. Then the musky odor of sour, unwashed bodies came to Hazzard's nostrils.

The imminence now of death was felt by Rima Van Dyke. She stepped close to Captain Hazzard and he felt the warmth of her trembling body close to his, could her efforts to breathe, almost could catch the poundings of her heart with his acute hearing. There was a soft click as Tyler Randall cocked his .45, chambering a round. All he needed was a target.

Captain Hazzard put out a steady hand, gave Rima's shoulder an encouraging touch. The light had been out for long seconds now, for it would only disclose their positions to the eyes hidden in the darkness.

There was a sudden opening of a door in the cabin of the dhow. Hazzard arrowed a beam from the flashlight toward the sound. He gasped. Rima caught her breath and sobbed in her throat. Randall cursed under his breath, swinging his gun hand up, looking for a reason to fire. In the open doorway stood a girl, now revealed by the small yellow beam. In her arms was a small monkey that clung to her ivory throat with both small hands. It was Azlea.

A terrible smile curved her cheery red lips, heightened the slant of her eyes, accentuated the full cheekbones. Captain Hazzard saw her womanly bosom rise and fall as with some great emotion, noticed her hands were tight fists. She stood tall and regal there in the doorway and the purpose of death was in every hard line of her beautiful face.

"Captain Hazzard – at last!" she spat out. Her lithe hands pulled the arms of the monkey from around her neck and the creature whimpered in fright, put small back hands over its face. Azlea rasped out

"No need to look for escape now. You are completely surrounded on all sides by over a hundred men. Even heaven and hell have moved against you! Turn the beam of your light upward for a moment and see for yourself."

With a quick flick of his wrist, Hazzard pointed the flash beam overhead. Rima gasped. Directly above and some ten feet over the wooden deck of the dhow half a dozen men hung at the ends of ropes.

Their fiendish eyes sparkled in the beam of the light and Hazzard saw the pointed tips of the kris blades they wielded.

There was a grating of noise of sliding wood. Captain Hazzard brought down the beam of the flash. Almost at their feet a sliding hatch had been pulled aside disclosing a well of darkness. Even as he looked, the wide stairs coming to the deck itself were filled with dacoits, flat-faced lascars. Each held either a short stabbing kris, or a crude club, ready for attack.

A chilling laugh made Hazzard look up. It was Azlea. Her face was strangely taut, and there was a near hysterical note in her brittle laughter, in the way her eyes gleamed.

"The great Captain Hazzard!" she taunted. "Made a fool of in front of the woman he loves! Well, Captain, why don't you work some of your miracles now!" She made a motion to the Dyak. "Now!"

On the instant a score of brown bodies charged at Captain Hazzard and his companions. His hard right fist found a dusky chin, and he heard the jaw crack under the blow. A whistling noise, he jerked his head back and a kris dagger bit into the deck inches from his boots. A gunshot cracked, followed by a piercing cry and a body smashed onto the deck.

Tyler Randall fired up on another of the pirates hanging overhead and was rewarded with another falling body. Meanwhile Captain Hazzard, started firing away with his own .45 at point blank range. One, two, three men fell over clutching bloody wounds. Rima screamed, unable to contain her fear any longer.

Before Hazzard could fire off another round, the press of Rima's army was on him and he began to use his pistol as a club, bashing in heads as long, dirty brown arms clawed up at him. He and the pilot desperately maneuvered the shaking girl between them, as the tide of killers threatened to overwhelm them. Once again Tyler Randall lost all semblance of humanity, as he struck out time and again, doing as much damage as his powerful fists could raining down constantly. He and Captain Hazzard fought like devils from hell, but as fast as they knocked a Dyak, his place was filled by others.

Something light brushed against Hazzard's throat. He paid no attention, aimed a blow at a pair of glaring eyes in front of him. Then something cut off his wind with the suddenness of a lightning bolt. He gasped, tore and clawed at the string of silk that cut deep into his bronzed throat. He knew then it was the end, the finish.

Thug stranglers had strings of silk about their necks!

As consciousness left Captain Hazzard, he had one thought, Rima. He was responsible for her, and now...? A well of blackness engulfed him...

Captain Hazzard fought back to consciousness. He thought he was in a morass of black quicksand, and it was choking him as he sank deeper into the quagmire with every step forward. He made the bank, fell on it, exhausted.

He opened his eyes, looked about him. An oil lamp glowed in his eyes, was gently swaying from a chain fastened to the ceiling. They were in a room located in the hold of the dhow. Hazzard tried to move, found he was fastened with iron wrist gyves. His arms were chained above his head.

He saw they had their backs – for Rima and Randall were likewise manacled – against the ribs of the dhow, the same long wrist bar holding all of them. Undoubtedly the dhow had been in the African slave trade, and this room they were in had been a prison for unruly blacks who protested leaving their native land.

Captain Hazzard quickly assessed their conditions. Both he and the blonde pilot were bruised and scratched up badly, their jackets were gone and what tatters remained of their shirts could hardly be called clothes. Whereas the girl had fared slightly better, only show a few smudges on her face and although her dress had been torn to reveal her stocking clad long legs, her blouse was whole.

Across the room was a stout door of black which Hazzard took to be teak. Above the door was a transom probably eight inches in height, the only opening. He heard a strangling noise from his left and knew it came from Tyler Randall. He strained his head outward, managed to see the aviator was regaining consciousness. Then, in a moment, Rima Van Dyke, who was shackled between them, shuddered, opened her eyes.

Captain Hazzard calmed her with his words of hope, telling her not to despair. The girl smiled at him and nodded. "I – I am not afraid," she claimed.

A sound of a chain clanking came from the direction of the door. It was pushed open, and a breath of cooler air eddied into the room. A man stood in the doorway. Behind him was Azlea. The man's swarthy face broke into a cruel smile as he surveyed Captain Hazzard. His red lips writhed into a wolfish smile and disclosed teeth white as bones. It was Nomar Samadi. Behind him was Azlea O'Hara, holding her furry pet, her head slightly bowed so as not to have to look at the chained prisoners.

"We meet at long last, Captain Hazzard," Samadi sneered.

He stepped into the room, strode to Hazzard. "Do you know who I am?"

"From the description, I assume you are the coward, Nomar Samadi."

A sadistic smile on his evil face, Samadi struck Captain Hazzard across the mouth. Blood spurted and coursed down Hazzard's chin.

Icy blue-gray eyes glared as Hazzard chuckled. "I was right. You are yellow."

The low, amused laughter suddenly infuriated the maddened Samadi. Again and again his brown fist flashed out, struck Hazzard's battered face, knocked his head from side to side. In the doorway, Azlea bit her lower lip as her nervous monkey jumped up and down in her arms, agitated by the renewed violence.

"Leave him alone!" Rima pleaded. "Please, stop hitting him!"

Tyler Randall strained his considerable strength at his wrist bonds, tried to kick out with his long legs, but the distance was too great. Samadi laughed now himself and there was more than an edge of madness to it. Panting heavily, he ceased the beating.

"Another few minutes, Captain, and you will be through. Your dead body will be thrown overboard. The girl and your friend will join you."

Captain Hazzard shook himself alert, spit out a gob of blood. "Why didn't you just finish the job when we were all unconscious?"

Samadi's obsidian eyes gleamed fiendishly. "Ha, a logical question. But murdering you while you were asleep would have robbed me. I will not grant you an easy death, Captain. You shall pay hard for those first victories of yours. No more will Nomar Samadi be laughed at. When you writhe in your chains, and scream for mercy, then Nomar Samadi will have his revenge."

Samadi thrusts his maddened face close to Hazzard. "You – all three of you – are to die the Cobra Death!"

A sob of terror came from Rima's throat. Captain Hazzard smiled at her and she subsided, became calm again. She said, her voice strained: "I am not afraid of Nomar Samadi. I wish father – send word to him – that I was not afraid. And then," her emotion almost overcame her, "I ask you to get word to Paul Dupres for me. A final request, please. Tell him I loved him, knew at the end he loved me as well. That is all, do as you wish." Her head drooped as merciful unconsciousness descended upon her.

"Paul Dupres!" Samadi laughed. "He is facing a different death even as I speak. The Coral Death!" He turned toward the door. "Mala – Talo! Come with my glass cage! Wheel in the Cobra Death! Let's see if the man who is supposed to have no fear can look my little pets in the eye!"

His maniacal laughter filled the room. The little monkey in Azlea's arms chattered and scolded in alarm clung to the girl's neck.

Captain Hazzard glanced at her, and what he saw brought a frown to his face. He saw a great struggle seething within her, saw that her terrible hatred of a moment before had been replaced by utter horror. She was trembling, was biting her crimson lips to keep them from forming a scream of terror.

And then a noise came from the room or passageway outside. It was if a piece of heavy furniture on casters was being pushed across an uneven floor. Azlea stepped hastily aside, her face white, eyes narrowed in loathing. And the Captain Hazzard knew why.

Through the doorway, pushed by two half-caste natives, a table on wheels rolled into the room. But it was a strange table, a table of horrible, unspeakable death.

On all for sides of the table were panes of heavy glass extending upward fully four feet. One of the panes of glass was arranged so it could be pulled up by means of a lever extending from the back of the table. This would leave a space of several feet between its lower edge and the top of the table. And now the reason for pulling up the pane of glass was too apparent to Captain Hazzard.

*"...all three of you...
are to die the Cobra Death!"*

For on that table, imprisoned by the walls of glass, were six king cobras!

The diabolical scheme was simple. The table was wheeled in front of Hazzard, the girl and Randall. It was only six inches away, the top level with Hazzard's waist. When Samadi raised the pane of glass the cobra would be unhampered, could strike at their unprotected faces!

"Samadi, no – no!"

The frenzied scream suddenly came from the writhing lips of Azlea O'Hara. She threw herself upon him, tried to hold his arm as it reached for the death lever of the glass cage. Her pet monkey dropped from her arms and scampered away out the door.

"You little fool! What are you doing?" he cried, and pushed her back.

"Please, do not kill him, Samadi, not – him!"

"Why the sudden change of heart?" the evil Samadi wanted to know. "A few minutes ago you were only too happy to see him suffer and die."

"But I didn't know," the girl sobbed. "The master lied to me when he said Captain Hazzard loved the – the white girl!"

"That is no concern of mine," Samadi said. "I have my orders and so do you. I suggest you stop this nonsense now."

Azlea bravely wiped the tears from her tanned cheeks and looked at the chained man she had come to admire, and even love to a certain degree. She had one card to play. She stepped in front of Nomar Samadi and slowly brought her hands up to his chest, smiled knowingly. "Earlier you made certain advances to me. Advances of love… and more."

"Which, as I recall," he touched the cheek she had slapped, "you rejected most emphatically. Now, because I am going to kill this man, you want to bargain for his life?"

Azlea looked up into his face, her eyes suggesting what her lips promised. "I can give you nights of pleasure beyond your wildest dreams, if you let him live."

Samadi suddenly started laughing again. Roughly he seized the girl's wrist and pulled them together. "Foolish little minx, don't your understand? Once I've taken care of Captain Hazzard and the others, our leader will grant me any boon I desire. Why should I bargain for what shall soon be mine freely?"

Fury filled Azlea's eyes and she spit in Samadi's face. "You fiend! I will never be yours. I would rather die first!"

Samadi signaled to his two men. "Get her out of her!" Mala and Talo, the half-castes, took hold of her arms and dragged the girl into the passageway outside. Captain Hazzard watched them go and vowed, should he survive, he would not forget what Azlea O'Hara had been willing to sacrifice for his life. But first, there was that matter of escape.

Nomar Samadi swerved on Hazzard, strode forward, his black eyes alight with utter madness. "Does your flesh crawl now, Captain Hazzard? Do the hairs on the back of your neck crinkle and quiver? Ah, fear is in your soul, withers your brain, your heart. You are mortally afraid now, you arrogant fool, for the Cobra Death soon will stab at your heart!"

But Captain Hazzard said nothing; his lips remained sealed.

Nomar Samadi screamed, struck Hazzard once more. He ran to the back of the table, jerked downward on the lever. The pane of glass swung up a full two feet. The writhing cobras within came erect, their extended hoods showing spectacled death's heads. And then, heads outthrust, fangs dripping amber poison, their sinuous bodies inched warily forward for the death strike.

A peal of insane laughter welling from his throat, Nomar Samadi turned and fled, slammed the door. Captain Hazzard heard the chain clank into place, sealing the room of the Cobra Death!

Chapter Seventeen
The Fate of
Jonathan Wells

Jonathan Wells knew he had one chance in a million of leaving his steaming cell alive. Yet he showed no fear.

His hellhole of concrete was as hot as a bake oven, and the narrow slit of an opening near the ceiling allowed no breeze from outside to enter. The door of the cell was of teakwood, almost as hard as cast iron. A rude bench, bolted to the floor, was the only furniture.

Several hours before, just as dark set in, Jonathan Wells was telephoned by a man claiming to Tyler Randall, Captain Hazzard's associate. He was told that Hazzard had uncovered amazing developments to the plot, that he then had the Red Maggot in his possession and Wells was to come to a certain estate near the Kalang Reservoir.

Jonathan Wells had hurried there without delay, noted fierce wild dogs roaming the grounds as he entered. He went into the house and was met by Nomar Samadi and a threatening gun.

Now he was in some dungeon-like cell beneath the house, a prisoner. From the slit in the concrete, which apparently led outside, he heard the snarls and whining cries of the fierce dholes as they roamed the grounds. Escape from that direction was impossible.

Men do not live long in the Far East before they acquire a feeling of fatalism. It is the creed of the East, one trait of the natives which the whites have no hesitancy in accepting.

Jonathan Wells was sixty-five years of age. From Munich he had come to Singapore and given the Van Dyke organization practically all of his business life. Now, in some rather indefinite way, he knew his long and honorable career was at an end. Just as the Far East breeds fatalism, so does it engineer courage. Jonathan Wells was not afraid.

And then, with startling suddenness, faint whisperings came to Jonathan Wells ears. They were mysterious, ethereal, seeming came from nowhere. His brown eyes narrowed and he looked about the small room. In a corner of the cubicle of concrete he saw something he had not noticed before.

It was a small round hole in the wall. He inspected it and decided that once a water pipe entered the cell. Long ago it had been removed, the iron pipe cut flush with the concrete wall and then plastered over. But the covering of plaster had not completely hidden the end of the pipe. A small hole allowed sounds from some room above to be heard in the cell, working on the same principle as a speaking tube.

By straining his ears, Jonathan Wells heard the voice of Nomar Samadi in conversation with some other man. He did not recognize this other voice when the man said to Samadi : "It is well, Samadi, that you should contemplate your many errors of the past. People who make errors do not work for me – long!"

There followed a long conversation, mention of the girl, Azlea. In a moment she had entered the room and Jonathan Wells heard the unknown voice taunt her with the falsehood that Captain Hazzard was in love with Rima Van Dyke. Being a close family friend, Wells was all too aware of Rima's feelings for Paul Dupres, the hardworking technician on Lost Island. It was a match both he and Otto Van Dyke approved of.

And then he heard of the murder plot to be orchestrated on the old dhow, the fact that Van Dyke himself had again been captured, was being flown to the coral island. Jonathan Wells knew the end was near – for him.

Strangely – this was a day of startling happenings – Jonathan Wells heard a hissing sound coming from the slit in the concrete which led to the outside grounds. He thought at first one of the wild dogs had winded him. But the hissing sound continued. Then Wells' heart leaped with sudden hope. For a soft voice in Malay said :

"Tuan Wells! It is Moh Tan. You will remember I once was your houseboy. I work here now, Tuan Wells, and I am afraid. This is an evil place. These people are fierce, do murder. I saw them capture you, take you to the cell."

"Moh Tan!" Wells remember a chubby-faced young man always anxious to do good work and get ahead. "But how did you get past the guard dogs?" Even excited, Jonathan Wells knew to keep his voice low.

"I am the one charged with their feeding, Tuan Wells, they know me so I was able to come to this little window unseen. Tell me what to do, Tuan, and I will do it!"

Jonathan Wells thoughts quickly how best to take advantage of the boy's offer. He could send him to the British police, but recalling the conversation he had just heard, there was the awful ambush on his friends that had to take priority of everything else. Even his own life.

"Listen carefully, Moh Tan. I have a pencil here and will write a note which you will deliver to – Captain Kevin Hazzard . You will find him at the Old Wharf, awaiting the yacht Cora Marie, which is due in port very shortly. Take this note to him, tell him to come without delay. I fear I do not have much time left."

He took a slip of paper from his pocket. He started to write when again whispers from the pipe attracted his attention. He listened and a look of incredible amazement overspread his tanned face. He knew the man behind this entire insidious affair!

Writing furiously, Jonathan Wells did not at first hear the footsteps descending the stairs in the passage outside his cell. Suddenly there was the sound of a key turning in the lock. Jonathan Wells jumped to his feet, but the message was not finished! It would have to do. He climbed up on the teak bench, pushed the paper through the little window, whispered fiercely:

"Run, Moh Tan – hurry!"

As Jonathan Wells feet touched the floor the door opened. He blinked for the sudden onslaught of light, which made a glaring corona around the figure of the man standing there. The fellow's face was hidden behind a garish island mask of coral pink silk. In his hand was an automatic which he pointed at the prisoner's heart.

"I know who you are!" Jonathan Wells announced, standing straight before his captor. His time had run out, but he would not die a coward. His proud face showing disdain, his chin thrust upward. His only prayer now was that Captain Hazzard would survive the villain's ambush and one day avenge him.

"It doesn't matter," the familiar voice calmly retorted. Then, without another word, the man pulled the trigger three times.

The sounds were a blasting thunder in the narrow confines of the small cell. Jonathan Wells, was thrown backwards into the concrete wall, then with a sigh, collapsed. He twitched once and was dead.

Chapter Eighteen
The Monkey
and the Snakes

Blue-gray eyes glazed as if with enamel at the slithering cobras. Captain Hazzard's being was filled with a nauseous loathing, but there was no stopping the clear thinking process of his intellect. And, as calmly as if he were planning a movement on a chess board, he began working out his strategy.

A cobra is the most vicious creature known to man. It is utterly fearless, will attack in the twinkling of an eye. Any movement, when the snake is erect and prepared to strike, will cause it to arrow forward, its death lunge often carrying the sinuous body forward several feet.

Randall, you must remain perfectly still! Captain Hazzard mentally warned his companion. Do you understand me? Relax your breathing and do not move. No matter what occurs!

Ten feet to his right, across from the comatose Rima Van Dyke, the shackled Tyler Randall rested his head back against the bulkhead and forced himself to look away from the six, coiled cobras. I understand, Captain, he replied via the telepathy Hazzard had taught him, but it isn't going to be easy.

Captain Hazzard knew that should he or Randall make any sudden movement one or more of the cobras would strike at their bodies, sink long fangs into flesh. Then would follow the chewing motion which most venomous reptiles have to make in order to sink their poison deep into the victim's veins. Then, in a few moments, death would follow.

At the moment, their only piece of good fortune was Rima's state of unconsciousness. Knowing Tyler Randall's make up from countless past exploits together, Captain Hazzard was confident he wouldn't panic, but remain cool and collected, even here in the face of an horrific death. Whereas if the girl awoke before he could devise a means of escape, she would surely begin screaming. Then all would be lost. So, if he were going to manufacture a plan, it had to be soon.

Just then a slight chattering noise was heard. Captain Hazzard, face stone rigid, looked up as the noise came again from the door. He stared, a puzzled look on his face. In the transom above the door was the gray form of the monkey, Azlea's pet.

Do you see it, Captain? Randall asked telepathically.

Yes. It could be our salvation. The monkey suddenly fell to floor and scampered across the floor and around the table with the deadly snakes.

Or our doom! Randall offered, if those cobras spot it!

Hazzard agreed, but there was nothing he could do about the pet's actions. Obviously Azlea had sent it. But for what purpose?

As the hairy little beast reached Hazzard, it stopped at his feet and looked up at him, the table from where the hissing cobras waited. Risking a glance, Hazzard tilted his head slowly downward. In the monkey's black hands was a key! The monkey started waving the key around and jumped up and down, once again starting its screeching.

The cobras were all agitated now, their flared, crown heads up and seeking the origin of the offending noise. Then the monkey climbed up Hazzard's left leg and came into full view of the nearest cobra. Captain Hazzard saw the snake raise up in the posture of attack. Its head starting to weave back and forth as the furry pet reached his left shoulder and raced up his left arm to deposit the key in his hand.

The cobra hissed one last time, as the harmless monkey returned to Hazzard's shoulder and for the first time became aware of the danger about to befall it. It froze on his shoulder, its small, round eyes caught in the cobra's mesmerizing stare. Captain Hazzard's mind feverishly calculated distances, the flexibility in the chains binding his arm and the trajectory of the venomous viper.

The cobra sprang up out of the glass case, fangs aimed at the quivering monkey. Captain Hazzard pulled his left arm in to his body and the snake struck the iron manacles around his wrist. It flopped to the floor like a fist out of water, where Hazzard immediately stomped down on its head, crushing it. The monkey clambered up onto his head and began waving its little arms, screaming at the remaining five cobras.

"Captain?" Tyler Randall having seen the blur of action out of the corner of his eye couldn't contain himself a second longer. "Did it get you?"

I'm fine, Randall! Don't say another word. We might just get out of this yet!

Without giving another thought to the remaining five snakes, now twisting about and hissing threatening at the annoying monkey, Captain Hazzard put the key in his mouth, held it tight with his teeth, twisted the manacle and slipped the key into the slot. A tight twist of his head and the iron bracelet fell away, fortuitously against his hip with a soft slap.

His left hand free, Captain Hazzard swiftly reached for one of the pouches on his utility belt. Thinking him defenseless without his gun, Nomar Samadi had not given his leather belt the slightest attention. If he had done so, he would have quickly removed it from the Captain's possession.

With sure movements he pulled out a tiny square of cloth padding in which was wrapped a small glass vial. He deftly removed the cloth with his fingers, with his forefinger flicked the little vial onto the table top. It landed in the midst of the writhing snakes with a tinkle of crushed glass. All five cobras turned, hissing horribly.

A glowing spot of red flames was created out of nothing. It grew, blossomed into a hellish red rose of fire, sputtered and spewed, and from it arose a single pencil of grayish smoke. It was a chemical flare of red which Captain Hazzard used for signaling purposes, much as a heliograph message is sent. The contents of the vial burst into hungry red flame as quickly as air reached it.

The Cobras writhed, unable to get away, as they were still surrounded on three sides by the glass panes. One of them struck at the ball of red, fell back as the terribly hot chemical burned through its venom-dripping mouth. Another struck, pushed the ball into the coils of its mate. The cobras thrashed about in the glass enclosure, made the table tremble with their death gyrations.

But one of the snakes glided forward, evading the fire, stuck an inquiring head of triangular horror toward Captain Hazzard's grim face. Its head and neck arced backward like a might spring. It was ready to strike.

Then another little ball of glass of thin glass made an almost invisible parabola, shattered on the table. From it a low-hanging gray gas sprang to life, rolled in little clouds across the table towards the weaving cobra. This was a blistering gas similar to mustard, entered the system through the skin pores or wherever moisture gathered.

It touched the sinuous body of the last cobra, caused the skin to raise into little mounds of blisters. The cobra writhed into a ball of horror, began to bite at its own body with vicious fangs.

And then, jarred loose by the cobras' wild movements, the lever slipped from its notch and the pane of glass crashed into place! Now all five cobras were quickly devoured by the chemical fire and soon their charred remains formed an ugly, sticking mound with the glass case.

Tyler Randall sighed, flashed a tremulous smile at Captain Hazzard. "Oh, boy!" was all he could say.

Captain Hazzard was busy unlocking his remaining manacle. He jerked, pushed outward, the wrist bracelet came free. He grabbed the monkey gently off his head and placed it back on the floor away from the dead snake he had crushed. Hazzard then proceeded to free Randall and together they unchained the still sleeping Rima Van Dyke.

As her manacles opened, she began to collapse and Randall caught her in his arms. "Chafe her arms," Captain Hazzard suggested, as he kicked the dead snake under the table. "Lucky for us, Miss O'Hara seems to have had a change of heart. It would appear she's on our side now! If we can get out the door ..."

A slight sound of metal outside the door was his answer. It swung slowly inward, and Azlea stood in the opening. The little monkey hurried to her, swung to her shoulder. She was breathing hard and spots of color showed in her olive cheeks. Her dark eyes were alight from some inner glow, some compelling force. Tyler Randall looked at her, then at Captain Hazzard and understood. He pitied this beautiful Eurasian girl who, for love of Captain Hazzard, risked her life.

"I managed to bring your guns," she whispered. "They're outside in the passageway. You must hurry! Samadi and his men are in the main cabin, drinking to your – deaths."

As Azlea O'Hara spoke, Rima slowly came awake. Seeing this, Randall set her down slowly until she was fully conscious. Seeing all of them standing by the door with the half-caste girl, Rima was smart enough not to utter a word, although her mind was awash with a hundred questions.

"Ah, the girl can walk," Azlea whispered. "Good. Follow me. There's a secret stair leading to the hatch overlooking the dock. I think you can make it if we go now."

"And what of you, Azlea?" Captain Hazzard asked softly. "Will you come with us?"

A wild light of hope flared in the girl's face and then died. She sighed, and when she spoke again her voice filled with resignation. "No. I will simply disappear if I win free with you. Heaven help me, I am a half-caste! I don't belong in either world." A sob tore from her clenched lips and tears glistened in her dark eyes.

Captain Hazzard, face flaming, gathered the girl's hands within his own, pressed them tenderly. He leaned forward and kissed her cheek. "That is not true, Azlea O'Hara. You will always have a place in my world."

Azlea looked up into his blue-gray eyes, and a brave and beautiful smile caused her face to become calm. "Your friendship gives me everything – everything!" Then her mood changed. "Quick!" she breathed. "We must hurry..."

Muffled shouts came from the passageway. Azlea screamed. Captain Hazzard pulled her lithe body behind him, leaped into the passageway. His fingers delved once more into his utility belt, came into view with several small, greenish oval shaped objects. There were tiny holes punctured in each of the strange balls that Hazzard called his Whistling Devils. He had been unable to use them when they had first entered the dhow because the Dyaks and lascars were too spread out on the open deck. But here in the confined spaces of the passageway, was different situation altogether.

He touched a button on one end of the first metal egg and a sputtering sounded in the strange thing's interior. Acid began to eat through a tinfoil outer shell. In a moment, when it touched another acid, a gas would be generated and pressure would built up. He threw Whistling Devil and it rolled down toward the horde of dacoits and lascars boiling down the narrow passage.

Suddenly a noxious gas erupted from the still rolling egg and then a loud, whining screech like that of a wailing banshee filled the air. The more gas escaped from the perforated holes, the faster the Whistling Devil whipped about until it was bouncing from wall to the other, creating a thick haze and screeching up a whirlwind of fury.

While the enemy was caught in the middle of this artificial tornado of sound and smoke, Azlea had retrieved their weapons and Captain Hazzard and Tyler Randall opened fire with their .45 automatics. Even though confused and afraid, some of the Dyaks found the courage to hurl their razor sharp krises through the thick smoke in hopes of hitting the escaping quartet.

Several of the thrown blades barely graced Captain Hazzard's body as he stood in that passageway of death and flung lead into the seething mass of flesh. Randall, at his side, was pulling the trigger methodically, but every leaden slug caused a death yell to twist from a dying man's throat. The enemy force was so crammed together, it was impossible for their shots not to hit something every time.

Captain Hazzard, seeing his first Whistling Devil was winding down, clicked the button on the second still in his hand and tossed it underhand. When it began to wail and discharge more foul smelling gas in the midst of the frenzied natives, this time they broke and ran. With Rima Van Dyke between them, Hazzard and Randall rushed forward. They made the end of the passage, jumping over fallen bodies as they went. Beyond lay the open deck. In a moment they were at the head of the gangplank.

Captain Hazzard turned.

"Azlea!" he called. "Hurry! Hurry!"

A powerful vibration shook the deck beneath their feet. Captain

Hazzard frowned. It was the sound of motors! The big dhow started to move away from the dock. The gangplank was about to fall into the water. Hazzard pushed Randall and the girl down the wobbling board, followed more slowly, still hoping to see the Eurasian girl. As he stepped to the dock the plank fell with a mighty splash. The dhow headed toward the open sea…

Captain Hazzard, Rima and Randall stood on the dark wharf and watched the dhow pull out into harbor. Hazzard said in hard, grating tones:

"I think we'll soon see Samadi again, Randall. He'll make for Lost Island and we must return there as well. The final showdown is ahead of us now. The Cora Marie will be here within the hour. We'll refuel, get the SeaBee hoisted aboard and turn back again…"

He stopped, swerved, and his hand went to his automatic. Captain Hazzard turned the beam of his flashlight up the wharf and it shone upon the staggering, nigh spent figure of a Malay. In his hand was a bit of rice paper which he held front of him.

"You are the one called Captain Hazzard?" the fellow gasped, about to collapse.

"Yes, I am. What have you got for me?" Hazzard help the man sit down on a crate near the end of the pier.

"It is a message from Tuan Wells. He – has – just – been killed."

"Oh, God, no!" Rima reacted, holding on to Randall for support.

"I am Moh Tan, a one time servant of Tuan Wells," the Malay continued, sweat beading his face. "As I fled with this note, I heard the shots – Tuan Well's death cry!"

Captain Hazzard unfolded the grim bit of paper, turned the beam of flash upon it. He read aloud:

"Trust Moh Tan. Have been captured by enemy. Moh Tan will lead you. Soon enemy leave for Lost Island by planes. Overhead their talk. Watch out for dhow ambush on Old Wharf. Herr Van Dyke kidnapped from hospital, already flown to island. Hurry. Enter island under sea. Man behind this is…"

The note ended. Captain Hazzard gently shook the Malay, questioned him in his own tongue to confirm what he had just read. Moh Tan nodded affirmatively to all of Hazzard's questions.

"What does he mean?" Rima blurted out, "that my father has been kidnapped again?"

"It is as I suspected, Rima. The mastermind behind this scheme wishes to bring us all to Lost Island for one final confrontation. Taking you father simply assures we will follow.

"And we shall, as God is my witness, make them pay for their crimes." Stray rays from the flashlight brought out his face in terrible relief. It was hard like steel, and Tyler Randall could see his blue-gray eyes almost black with intensity, the scar livid over his left eye.

Captain Hazzard said, and the simple words were a prayer : "Heaven rest his brave soul! Jonathan Wells is dead!"

Chapter Nineteen
Beneath the Waves

The Cora Marie docked approximately an hour later. By that time, Captain Hazzard and Tyler Randall had made a few calls to the proper authorities and commissioned a fuel tanker to be ready when Thomas Floyd's magnificent yacht slipped into her berth.

The second the ship's engines were silences and her mooring lines made taut, First Mate Hank Carter jumped onto the pier and began overseeing the refueling operation without delay.

Aboard the Cora Marie, Captain Hazzard sketched briefly what had happened since their flight into Singapore to Floyd and a very anxious Jake Cole. Meanwhile Randall had escorted Rima Van Dyke to her cabin, the girl was shaken and weeping. Her ordeal was far from over.

"So what's the plan, Chief?" the happy cowboy spoke around a thick wad of chewing gum. They were in the main salon drinking coffee and having a quick breakfast. Once Hazzard had completed his report, the Montana wrangler was eager to get into action. The dull routine of the past few days had been pure torture for him.

"Rest easy, Jake," Captain Hazzard said as Randall came into the cabin to join them. "Once the ship is refueled, we have to get the Seabee and hoist her back onto her catapult. She proved an invaluable asset and I don't want to sail without her."

"Right you are," Thomas Floyd beamed, happy to know his speedy little airplane had been of use to his friends. "All this shouldn't take more than few hours, tops."

"Excellent." Captain Hazzard looked at all their faces and was silently grateful to have such stalwart companions. With them at his side, there was no villainy he would not challenge. "Gentlemen, I suggest we get as much rest as possible during the next few days of our voyage. Once we reach Otto Van Dyke's Lost Island, the goal before us will be a very dangerous one.

"Not only must we learn his location, and that of his chief supervisor, Paul Dupres, and rescue them, but we must all seek out this faceless mastermind whose bloody hands reach from America to these beautiful shores. We must unmask him and then defeat him, once and for all!"

"Here, here!" Thomas Floyd took his feet and clapped his hands. "Well spoken, Hazzard! I'm with you all the way, my friend!"

Kevin Douglas Hazzard looked at the explorer and the willing faces of Jake Cole and Tyler Randall and expected no other answer.

****

The first horizontal rays of sunlight were slanting across bustling Singapore harbor when the Cora Marie put to sea, mighty diesel engines at full throttle. Shortly afterward, but a speck on the horizon, the city disappeared from view.

Having showered and changed into clean clothes, Captain Hazzard returned to the deck of the swift craft. Face tense, his blue-gray eyes were hard, wintry as the cool sea air hit him full on. He stood relaxed in the bow of the plunging yacht watching unbroken swell of water pass beneath the prow. The death of Jonathan Wells had been a personal one. He deeply admired this little man who, under the sentence of death, had died as only brave men die.

He wished he could have stayed in Singapore with Jubal Beck and help pay his last respects. Wells' body had been found in the abandoned house by the Kalang Reservoir, the noble Malay, Mon Tan, having guided the British Police to its location. Unfortunately, except for the wild dogs and the corpse, the old house was empty, its master having long fled before the police raid could nab him.

Beck had promised Captain Hazzard that Jonathan Wells received every attention in those last earthy rites. Later, the manager of Van Dyke enterprises, said he would charter a private plane and meet the Cora Marie at Lost Island, to fight shoulder to shoulder with the others to protect Otto Van Dyke, now Nomar Samadi's prisoner there.

Captain Hazzard wondered about Azlea O'Hara. His handsome face softened at the memory of her sacrifice. He wondered if Samadi had killed her for her role in their escape from the dhow. Again his face hardened. It was another score to settle with the dark man and his gang. There was Paul Dupres, too. Rima loved him. He too, was a prisoner of the island, perhaps dead by now. Hazzard slammed a hard fist into the palm of his left hand.

There were many scores to settle!

Then he remembered the message from the dead Jonathan Wells. "Enter island under sea," he had written. He had overheard of the secret entrance before he died. He knew that Captain Hazzard had a bathysphere aboard the yacht, had been told of the self-contained diving suits.

The secret entrance was the island's weak spot. Jonathan Wells knew it probably could be captured with a surprise attack if entered from underwater!

He would bring Jake Cole with him on the underwater assault. Hazzard was determined to capture Lost Island.

All day and the following night the mighty propeller and twin screws of the Cora Marie forced her westward toward the Java Sea. They passed the tip of Borneo, the mouth of the sluggish Barito, reached the Java Sea.

That night, after another fabulous dinner served up by stout little Manuel Ramirez, Captain Hazzard assembled Jake Cole and Tyler Randall on the fantail stern. The night heavens were filled with stars. Back in the salon, Thomas Floyd had sat down at his grand piano to entertain the still weary jewelers daughter.

"Tomorrow we reach Lost Island," Hazzard began. "I've laid out a plan of attack that takes into account all those things we've learned about our elusive foes."

Jack Cole stuck a piece of chewing gum in his mouth and leaned back against the stern rail behind the bathysphere. "So, what you got up your sleeve, Boss?" he grinned.

"We know two things for certain," Captain Hazzard began. "One, that somewhere on that ragged island, Otto Van Dyke and Paul Dupres are either dead or being held prisoner. Two, there is a secret underwater passage into island."

"Because of the mysterious diver who attacked you before," Randall concluded.

"Exactly. Which explains what happened in the cove after we had flown off."

"Hot-doggies!" the cowboy pulled off his Stetson and slapped his right leg with it. "That's how them oil barrels suddenly popped up so close to us without anyone seeing them!"

"That is the only assumption that works," Hazzard continued. "That same diver must have dragged a fuel drum through the secret passage way with weights affixed to it. Upon reaching the area beneath the ship, he released the contents it floated to the surface. As it did so he would have used some kind of underwater torch to ignite this oil and thus created the fire that suddenly appeared in the water."

"I think you've got it, Chief," Cole's eyes were bright, remembering the events that had forced them to abandon the cove and cast off for Singapore.

"And that seadog must let the can go once he got his fire lit. We all spotted it bobbing near the hottest flames.

"Why, he must have been looking up at us from the bottom, all the time we was running around like chickens with their heads lopped off! Tarnation, they're a wily bunch alright!"

"Exactly, Jake, which is why we must not underestimate them a second time."

"You think they'll come at us from below again?" Tyler Randall asked.

"It worked for them before," Hazzard said. "It's a good bet they will do so again. As long as the Cora Marie is at anchor, she'll be vulnerable to such an attack."

"So, how do we stop them?"

"By staying in touch our special way," Captain Hazzard touched his forehead, smiled. "Jake is going to come with me in the bathysphere to find the secret entrance. You, Randall, will remain aboard and ever vigilant for any kind of underwater activity that might prove a threat to the ship."

"You really think those varmints are going to come after us?" Cole wanted to know. The anticipation of a good brawl was getting him wound up.

Captain Hazzard stepped up to the railing and looked out over the white wash being left by the ship's twin props. The sea looked calm and serene but in his mind were concerns for the dangers they would soon face with the rising sun.

"Yes, I do," he replied softly. "And I we will be ready for them this time."

As dawn marches across the turquoise waters, a dim dot showed on the horizon, grew larger as the crew watched. It was Lost Island.

An hour later the Cora Marie was hove to the island's lee, the side on which the bathysphere lay concealed completely hidden from view.

While everyone ate a hasty breakfast, the bathysphere was made ready for a dive. Fearful of an attack on the actual ship, Captain Hazzard had decided to manipulate both Thomas Floyd and Rima Van Dyke to a place of abject safety. He invited them to join Jake Cole and himself on the dive. Of course he said nothing of his intentions to find the secret underway passage. Besides he hoped the dive would cause the girl to momentarily forget her father's plight, that the novelty of it would bring her some ease of mind.

Caught off guard, the girl agreed to join them. As for Skipper Floyd, he was only too happy to explore the sea floor. After all, he still had his assignment for the museum to carry out.

The bathysphere's door was clamped shut, and Captain Hazzard tested the air supply. Thomas Floyd sat beside him at the control bench, while Cole and the girl stood behind them, holding on to the leather-hand straps to either side of the cramped space. The cowboy had left his Stetson back in his cabin and felt naked without it sitting atop his head.

Through the quartz glass, Captain Hazzard signaled Hank Carter to lower away. Beyond the sailor, Tyler Randall, right hand on his .45 automatic, waved to Hazzard. Take care, Captain, he mentally sent as the big steel ball was lowered into the clear blue water.

A misty haze hung over the island and below it was shadowy, silent death. Strange fish flashed past the fused quartz windows and brought exclamations of delight from both Rima Van Dyke and Jake Cole. But Captain Hazzard noted something strange about their swift passage.

They did not float past in lazy contemplation, stop and stare through bulging eyes at this unusual round ball from another world. They swam fast, as if they were startled, as if some other enemy lurked in the shadows cast by the precipitous coral cliffs.

Eyes hard, like glazed steel, Captain Hazzard sensed danger was near. He nudged the cowboy and they passed into the pressure chamber in which hung the four diving suits. They aided each other into donning two of the cumbersome suits.

"I feel like one of them processed hot dogs," Jake Cole laughed, popping the new wad of gum in his mouth, as Hazzard slid the helmet over his head.

Before donning his own, Captain Hazzard opened the sliding door which led into the other segment of the bathysphere. Rima stared at him with surprise in her eyes. He grinned reassuringly at her, turned to the explorer.

"Jake and I are going out for a few minutes, Floyd. I want to look at something I spotted in my first dive."

"But," the explorer argued, "there's no need of your risking your lives out there!" He jerked his thumb at the watery depths. "We should get back aboard the Cora Marie. It's broad daylight now, and we've got to get on that island!"

Realizing there was no way to get around it, in terse words, Captain Hazzard explained the true nature of his actions. He meant to enter the island by the secret entrance, try to capture it with Cole's assistance.

"Randall is fully aware of my plan of attack and will give you all the details. Signal Carter to draw you up as we leave the pressure chamber. There could possibly be… Look!"

He pointed out the quartz window. Thomas Floyd and Rima turned, and a cry of horror sprang from her throat. Advancing on the bathysphere, a curious rod-like thing in his hands, was the mysterious diver!

Captain Hazzard returned to the chamber and leaning into Jake Cole, yelled so that he could hear, "We've got company out there!"

Through his glass face plate, the Montana wrangler grinned wide. He then began to twist the clamps that sealed the door while Hazzard affixed his own helmet and clamped on heavy lead shoes. Once done, Captain Hazzard quickly twisted valves and sea water began gushing into the chamber. Other valves built up the air pressure so it approximated that of the depths.

Finally, Hazzard opened the outer door and followed by Cole, stepped from the bathysphere onto the bed of the Java Sea.

The champion of justice had immediately recognized that rod-like instrument carried by the villainous diver. It was an underwater cutting torch such as salvage crews use in cutting up a sunken ship so it may be draw up piecemeal. The diver planned to cut the hoisting lines of the bathysphere, maroon them on the bottom of the sea!

Captain Hazzard and Jake Cole moved in opposite directions to circumnavigate the giant steel ball and find their foe before he could achieve his goal. Hazzard came upon him first, seeing a brilliant white light above the bathysphere. The diver had pulled himself up along the outer shell using the ladder rung welded there, raised his cutting torch and even as Captain Hazzard watched, the hoisting lines of the steel ball parted! Hazzard moved forward as fast as the weight of his suit and the terrific pressure would allow.

On the other side of the bathysphere, Jake Cole was shocked to see the giant ball suddenly tilt towards him as it began to rollover. Digging his booted feet into the cloying, sandy bottom, he pushed with his legs for all he was worth. The hull of the bathysphere slammed into his back just as he was propelling himself away from it, the impact pushing him over a bowling candlepin.

Again came a burst of bubbles, then roiling of the water, as silt kicked up from the bottom enveloped Captain Hazzard. Helpless, he stood motionless waiting for it to resettle. The bubbles ceased and the diver had vanished!

Captain Hazzard turned toward the bathysphere, and a cry of fear for his companion sounded hollow in the confines of the helmet. He watched in horror as the bathysphere, released of its hoisting wire, was slowly turning over!

Then it seemed to stop. Captain Hazzard lunged forward, moving as fast as he could around the giant ball, his mind feverish with what he would find on the other side. There was Jake Cole, booted feet almost ankle deep in the sea floor, holding back the bathysphere from rolling any further. A cry of joy escaped from Hazzard as he hurriedly got into position alongside the struggling Cole, leaning backwards as to get his mighty shoulders against the slippery steel, pushed with all his strength.

Sensing the tremendous weight of the bathysphere had lessened against him, Jake Cole turned his head and saw Hazzard beside him. All was not lost yet. He renewed his own efforts to push back the mighty sphere.

Captain Hazzard twisted about and discovered one of the quartz windows of the ball was almost directly in front of his helmet. Within the bathysphere he saw Floyd and Rima, the latter terror-stricken. But the explorer's face lit up when he saw Hazzard peering through the quartz.

Using one free hand as much as possible, Captain Hazzard motioned to his own diving helmet, then pointed to Rim Van Dyke and Floyd. But his efforts, like Cole's, to obtain purchase for his feet stirred up muddy silt again, obstructed his view of the interior of the bathysphere.

After what seemed like long minutes of effort, Captain Hazzard made the explorer get his meaning. Thomas Floyd nodded, and Hazzard saw him turn and speak swift words to the girl. Captain Hazzard grinned in taut satisfaction. Floyd understood.

Captain Hazzard's great muscular shoulders strained almost to the point of breaking and Jake Cole's wiry tenacity, held the bathysphere level. Through the quartz window they saw Floyd help Rima don a diving suit, then climb into his own. Hazzard knew the air in the diving ball was becoming thin, soon would be nonexistent, heavily charged with carbon monoxide. Their only safety was in the diving suits!

The bathysphere rolled a bit. The cowboy dug his feet into new depressions of the bottom, while Captain Hazzard thrust again with his shoulders and together they kept it from turning. Should it roll a few more inches, it would be impossible for the two inside to open the outside pressure door; they would be doomed within the steel prison!

Flashing out desperate messages of "Hurry – hurry!" Captain Hazzard strained for purchase, so his shoulders would not slip. Through Cole's faceplate, he could see the cowboy's straining grimace, beads of sweat dotting his lean face.

And then, just when the physical endurance of these amazing men could no longer hold out, the outer door opened and Thomas Floyd and Rima Van Dyke tumbled from the bathysphere. Once they were both a safe distance in the clear, Captain Hazzard motioned Jake Cole to move aside, leaped away from the turning sphere of steel. It settled slowly between them, lay so that the door of the pressure chamber, although now open, was almost flat against the bed of the ocean.

Captain Hazzard rested momentarily against the steel shell of the bathysphere. Jake Cole was on his knees a few yards away, catching his own breath. Hazzard looked around, and a taut smile parted his lips. He bent, picked up a half shell which had somehow been left there.

Coral growths were all around them like an eerie, forest of fantasy.

Hazzard regulated his breathing, closed his eyes and mentally sent Tyler Randall a message. Through the use of his telepathic abilities, he informed the pilot of their narrow escape from the fiendish diver's attack and that the bathysphere was now unattached to the cables.

What do you want me to do, Captain? Randall's thought-message came in loud and clear. Hazzard responded, Raise the hoist cable and set about repairing the severed end. Then remain alert for any further attacks. We will set about finding the secret entrance to Lost Island.

After sending this command, Captain Hazzard moved away from the bathysphere and joined Rima Van Dyke and Thomas Floyd. A few minutes later the hoist cables began to show movement and then were gone, pulled back to the surface world. Something they could not do. Their only hope of surviving was to find the secret entrance to the coral island.

Captain Hazzard waved to Cole who rose up and waved back that he was ready to go. Weaving with fatigue, every pore exuding profuse perspiration, Hazzard motioned for the girl to get between him and the explorer. Jake would take up the rear. He took her hand, led them toward the black shadows of the coral cliffs.

Captain Hazzard knew that nearby lay some means of entrance into the center of the island. Jonathan Wells final message had confirmed that fact. But where it was he had no idea. But there could be little delay now. He, and Jake, had used up half their air supply in the terrible exertion of keeping the bathysphere from rolling. Escape had to be near...

For long minutes, Captain Hazzard searched the blackness, hands groping for some hole, some entrance way. He felt the air becoming thin in his diving suit. He was becoming groggy, thick-headed for lack of oxygen for his straining lungs. His hand went to the emergency supply and twisted the tiny valve. New vigor flowed into his veins as the pure air was drawn into his lungs. He was pleased to see Cole copying his actions.

He stumbled onward. The steel of purpose filled him, strengthened his lagging muscles. And then, when again the air was becoming thin and his strength ebbed from his muscles, he fell over a low shelf of coral. His fumbling hands found another shelf, still another. It was a stairway hewn into the coral of the Lost Island!

Gasping, every taut muscle straining, his heart hammering and blood pounding in his temples, Captain Hazzard toiled upward step by step. It was agonizing, a labor threatening to end as each higher step was reached.

It took long and precious seconds for him to understand why his feet were so heavy, why the diving suit became a near unsupportable burden. He was leading them nearer the surface where the pressure was not so great but the weight of the diving suits was greater in proportion to their closeness to the surface!

Escape, now was but a few steps above them. Suddenly he sensed Rima lose her footing behind him and fall backwards. Thomas Floyd managed to grab her arm as she dropped past him and hold on. Below, in the inky darkness, Jake Cole felt the girl's other arm and was quick to catch her. Using all the remaining stamina he could muster, he pushed up the coral path, bringing her back to a standing position beside the exhausted explorer.

Rima's fall only accentuated Captain Hazzard's true fears. He had no fear of his own death, but the responsibility of the girl, the explorer and the cowboy weighed heavily upon him. He must win free for them. And to eradicate forever the menace of the Red Maggot.

With clumsy fingers he unbuckled the heavy leaden shoes and stepped out of them, motioning the others to do likewise. Cole and Floyd did their own then aided the girl. Strangely, the effort helped Hazzard, for now he took four or five of the slippery coral steps with newfound strength. But the terrific exertion, he knew, was almost beyond his endurance.

He was crawling now, on weaving hands and knees. He reached upward, jerked back his hand. A warm something had touched his hand. And then he knew. It was air! He was at the surface! They had escaped!

With his final strength, Captain Hazzard helped draw Rima up the last shelf of coral. With desperate hands he unclamped her heavy helmet, tore it from her head. He saw she was white, almost trance-like with fear. He removed the helmet from Floyd's suit, heard it strike the coral with a metallic clang. Next he tackled Cole's, happy to see the cowboy's sweaty face smiling as the heavy iron helmet came off. Then he worked upon his own helmet, Jake assisted in unfastening the clamps for him.

Sweet, fresh air rushed into his face like a blow. He sucked it into his mouth, felt his flattened lungs fill out, the blood rush through his veins. He smiled, lay supine next to Jake Cole.

"Sakes alive," Cole exclaimed. "I never thought air could taste so darn good!"

"Amen to that," coughed Thomas Floyd. "Breathing is a habit I've come to appreciate over the years. I'd hate to give it up now."

All of them laughed weakly. Captain Hazzard, revitalized, sat up, looked at Rima Van Dyke. He touched her cheek, felt the warmth of her blood as it rushed to her face. She was safe.

"I'm fine," she whispered, still conserving her strength. "Thanks to you and Jake. You saved our lives down there."

A faint sound came to Hazzard's sensitive ears. He started, twist-

"Welcome to Lost Island, Captain Hazzard!"
Samadi sneered."

ed about, and a gasp of surprise welled from his throat.

Behind them, an automatic clasped in his long fingers, stood No-mar Samadi! Behind him were four Dyaks, their krises out, ready for attack.

"Welcome to Lost Island, Captain Hazzard!" Samadi sneered. "I have been expecting you. Now at long last you have come. Racing to your end… this time!"

He stepped forward, his wolfish grin of triumph showing his white teeth, the madness in his black eyes.

Chapter Twenty
Prisoners of Lost Island

Trapped, unarmed, weak from exhaustion, Captain Hazzard, Jake Cole and Thomas Floyd submitted to a weapons search without a struggle. First they were allowed to remove their cumbersome diving suits and then Samadi examined each of them personally. His one shred of decency was exempting Rima Van Dyke from such an indignity. The search was a thorough one, but Samadi failed to comprehend the purpose of Hazzard's military utility belt and its many pouches. Nor did he discover that the heels of Hazzard's boots could be taken off with a quick twist.

Herded before Samadi and his four natives, the three men and Rima were marched upward through a winding passageway hewn from the coral. The underground room they had just vacated was slightly higher than the water level. The coral was a deep pink, glistened like the first red flush of the sun over the Java Sea.

Above them, fully fifty yards along an upward slanting gallery, they came to a large room. It was furnished with a large table, many chairs and a bed in one corner of the room. A telephone reposed on the desk, or table.

"This is the central room occupied by…" Samadi laughed. He nodded to the Malays and they bowed and left. Samadi, automatic ready, guarded the four interlopers. "But wait, here is your host now."

Footsteps sounded from across the room. Captain Hazzard drew a deep breath. He knew that now he was to see the man who was behind the death plots, who had stolen the Red Maggot in order that he might rule the superstitious natives, eventually win untold treasures through the manufacture of the pearls. To foment, perhaps, unrest, rebellion – to drive the whites from the South Seas so he could rule them dictatorially.

A man entered the room. Hazzard stared. The newcomer wore a brown hood that covered his face except for two eye-holes! The rest of his garb was familiar light weight khaki as worn by most foreigners to the islands. He stood for a moment, this masked man, surveying his three captives.

Then a laugh of sneering triumph issued from behind the hood. He suddenly struck his hands together, and two fierce Dyaks came from the passageway behind, took up their guard in absolute silence.

"Welcome, visitors to Lost Island," the masked man said in a thin, reedy voice.

Captain Hazzard started. That voice was vaguely familiar to his acute sense of hearing. Still he was not able to place it just yet. He knew the hooded man was talking in a higher pitch than normally used, was disguising it.

"There are many strange and beautiful things here, Captain Hazzard." His laugh was sneering, at his own feigned politeness. "Death is here, too, and even death can be beautiful as all of you will soon discover!

"You have thwarted me many times these past few months, but this is the end for you, Captain. Jonathan Wells died, Otto Van Dyke and Paul Dupres are soon to follow him." The hooded mastermind waved his finger at Hazzard. "Samadi, here, tells me you had no fear when the king cobras were loosed almost at your throat. He tells me you have no fear of anything! We shall see, my good Captain, we shall surely see!"

He laugh continued keen, knifed the room like a whiplash. He resumed : "Yes, this is a strange island. At the foot of these cliffs untold hundreds of first water pearls lie in virgin shell. It was while diving for them that we found the underwater entrance.

"But now we go nature one better. We make pearls, priceless ones that cannot be told from the genuine! Already I have made millions by flooding the pearl markets of the world with these. I shall make many more millions before I am finished.

"I have the Red Maggot now, Captain Hazzard. I soon will be ready to incite the natives to action, cause them to rise in their superstitious zeal and drive the whites from the South Seas. I shall rule over them myself.

"But something else about the island. That fool, Van Dyke, didn't know that when he discovered a way to make pearls he also, by the same process, could make coral! As you know, coral is made of the skeletons of little animals called polyps. By forcing carbonate of lime into electrically charged sea water we cause the microscopic creature to die faster, thus build up coral.

"And," his laugh was shrill with mad hatred as he paced before his captives – "you should see the Coral Death! Three people are undergoing it even as we speak. Mr. Otto Van Dyke himself, Paul Dupres and – Azlea O'Hara!"

Captain Hazzard took a step forward, a menacing growl erupting from his throat, the light scar over his eye deepening in shade. The knife wielding Dyaks stepped between him and their master. The hooded villain had jumped back, forgetting Hazzard was at the mercy of the gun-toting Nomar Samadi. He approached again and waved his fist in Hazzard's face threateningly.

"Yes, I have her, who betrayed me by allowing you to escape from the room of king cobras! She will pay this debt to me with her very life!"

"Don't put down that gun," Captain Hazzard warned. "Because if you, I promise I will break your neck with my bare hands."

"Let me shoot him now!" Nomar Samadi begged the hooded man. "He's too dangerous to keep alive!"

"Quiet, you fool," the leader snapped. "We will do things my way!"

"My father!" cried a grief stricken Rima Van Dyke. "You fiend! Please, I beg of you, let me see him just once?"

The masked criminal diverted his attention to the frightened blonde. "You will all get to speak with them shortly. For now, Captain," he waved his pistol towards an alcove cut in the coral wall, "please, step this way. I have something to show you."

Eyes narrowed, Captain Hazzard's gaze followed the masked man's pointing gesture. He saw how light came into this small, inner chamber. Small square holes were cut into the coral, and daylight streamed through!

He walked over to one of the holes, looked out. Then he understood.

The alcove had been hollowed away so that only a thin barrier wall was left standing. Then the holes had been cut. Hazzard looked down, saw beneath him the deck of the Cora Marie!

The cliff of coral was similar to the Rock of Gibraltar which has passages and rooms carved out within it, peepholes so that those in the passages may watch the ships steaming past. The coral cliffs of Lost Island had served the same purpose. Captain Hazzard did not wonder now why those of the island knew his every movement aboard the yacht. He felt almost as if he could reach down and touch it.

He saw Tyler Randall, the aviator, and members of the crew pacing distractedly up and down the deck near the empty space where the bathysphere had rested. Of them, only Randall knew they were not still within the steel ball marooned on the bed of the ocean. Hazzard had cautioned him to keep their escape from that watery grave to himself fearing the boat was under close watch. Now that hunch had been proven out.

"Look closely, Captain," said the hooded man's reedy voice. Captain Hazzard saw him wink at Nomar Samadi. "Even now my experienced diver is rising under the yacht, his electric cutting torch ready. Before those on the ship know what is happening it will sink beneath them!"

Hazzard showed no reaction. He knew what the hooded fiend threatened was all too true. The keel plates of the Cora Marie could be cut. If that were to happen, she was would sink instantly.

But there was a smile of triumph on the handsome face of Captain Hazzard as he peered through the hole in the coral at the deck of the Cora Marie. Calming his mind, he silently sent out an alarm to Tyler Randall.

Randall, beware! Hazzard sent forth through the ether. *The mysterious diver is below the ship and about to sabotage her! You must act swiftly and stop him!*

Hazzard was rewarded instantly when he saw Randall suddenly bolt into the main cabin. A few seconds later the tall, blonde pilot re-emerged followed by the First Mate Hank Carter and the cook, Manuel Ramirez. Randall had removed his boots and shirts, draped around his neck was a pair of diving goggles. Randall pulled up the goggles over his face, adjusted them snuggly over his eyes and then opened his hand to Ramirez to accept one final item. Captain Hazzard squinted and recognized a long steel butcher knife being transferred to Randall. His companion placed the deadly blade between his teeth, climbed over the portside railing and smoothly dived into the shimmering blue-green water.

"What's going on down there?" the masked villain yelled in an agitated voice, forgetting to disguise it. "Why did that man jump into the water?"

Nomar Samadi came up behind Hazzard. "What is going on? Have they discovered our diver, LaPorte?"

"But how could they?" the master wailed, now clearly frantic. He pushed at Hazzard's chest. "HOW?"

Chapter Twenty-One
A Gruesome End

Tyler Randall sliced through the warm waters and, kicking with his bare feet, propelled himself around the curvature of the hull. If there was a diver beneath the keel, he would spot him easily enough, the water being clear like glass.

The first giveaway was a small stream of air bubbles rising up from the keel. Randall knew they came from a breathing tank. He kicked faster, his long arms stroking smoothly.

He sighted the deep-sea saboteur just in time, as the rogue was just about to raise his electric cutting torch to the steel belly of the Cora Marie. Randall's eyes, through the goggle lenses blinked at the brilliant fire on the tip of the long rod. It was only a few feet from the hull.

Tyler Randall took the knife from his teeth and went after the helmeted diver. He had hoped to reach him before the other realized he had company. Unfortunately that was not to be, as the diver was looking in his direction and Randall Tyler was a very big man. The surprised diver, eyes wide, pulled the cutting rod away from the ship and swinging it around, held it out towards the oncoming swimmer.

Frantically Randall twisted his long body away from the burning tip of the rod and dove away just barely missing it. He could feel heat from the glowing red end as his legs kicked hard away. Of course being unencumbered with a full diving suit and helmet, Randall had the advantage of maneuverability in this contest beneath the waves. What he lacked was air to sustain a lengthy encounter.

If he was to defeat the diver, it would have to be quickly. All this ran through his thoughts as he knifed his body around and sway for all he was worth below the lead-weighted boots of his opponent. The diver, rod held tightly in his hands, was trying to lower his helmet to keep the agile swimmer in his view, but it was impossible.

Tyler Randall rose up behind the desperate diver and before the fellow could turn, reached out and grabbed hold of the air tank affixed to the shoulders of his leather suit. Feeling Randall's hold, the diver tried to twist around and bring his lethal electric staff into play again. Randall wasn't about to let him have that second chance. He brought the knife down on the rubber tubes that connected the air supply to the back of the helmet and cut through them. Bubbles spewed out from the ruined tubes and the diver became frantic.

Randall swam away backwards and watched as the diver tried in vain to reach over his shoulder. Desperate to stay alive, the electric cutting torch was forgotten and dropped out of his hands to drift away towards the sea floor. The diver's body was twisting about crazily as the air continued to escape from his tank.

Suddenly a huge black shadow passed over Tyler Randall and went straight for the struggling diver. The man, LaPorte, drowning slowly, was still conscious enough to see the killing machine that was coming for him. A ten foot great white shark tore into him, its ugly maw opening and taking hold of his right leg. Blood erupted everywhere as the silent killer of the deep ripped the leg away, boot and all.

Fully aware that the scent of fresh blood would bring other sharks, Tyler Randall swam as fast as his legs and arms could move him for the surface. The second he broke into the warm, humid air, he began climbing the wooden ladder draped over the side. Behind a huge area of sea had started to turn red. In the distance several familiar fins approached, cutting through the water swiftly.

"By Neptune's beard," Hank Carter gasped, helping Randall over the railing. "What happened down there?"

"I found the enemy diver," answered Randall, removing his goggles and taking a towel from the cook, Ramirez. "And so did a great white."

The fat, little Mexican registered Randall's story, looked back at the water and the boiling activity now occurring and his face took on a sickly pallor. He quickly crossed himself and stepped away from the side.

"But I still don't understand how you knew that fellah was down below us?" the first mate said scratching his chin. "And what about the Skipper and the others in the diving ball? What if that scallywag did them foul?"

Shaking his mane of blonde hair, Tyler Randall took a deep breath and then eyed Hank Carter squarely. "I know you are going to have trouble believing this, Carter, but Captain Hazzard and the others are no longer in the bathysphere."

"What?" Now total confusion washed over the sailor's sour face. "I don't get what you're saying, mate? Speak English, will yah?"

"Raise the cables, Carter," Randall directed. "You'll discover they have been cut and are no longer attached to the bathysphere."

Alarm replaced the man's perplexed expression as he dashed to the ship's stern and gave orders to the crewmen to crank up the heavy cables. A few short minutes later the severed ends of the coated lines popped out of the water and dangled over their heads attesting to the truth of the pilot's claim.

All the while Tyler Randall was in direct telepathic contact with Captain Hazzard, having informed him of his battle with the diver and its gruesome outcome. Now Hazzard was repeating an earlier order. Stick to our original plan, Randall. You must find the enemy's hidden harbor! We may not have much time left!

"Carter, we've got to weigh anchor and get the hell out of here!"

"But where's the Skipper?"

Roughly the huge aviator took the first mate by the arm and pulled him away from the already nervous crew. Mumblings were heard about those in the bathysphere having drowned and nothing but bad luck had befallen them since coming to these cursed waters. Randall could sense panic creeping in and he had to take control or all would be lost.

"Listen to me carefully," he said, lowering his voice so only Carter could hear him. "Our friends are all prisoners on Lost Island."

"But how…"

"Shut up and listen to me, man! I have no time to explain everything. Our friends are in danger and unless you do exactly as I say, they will die."

Carter's mouth shut tight.

"Is that clear enough for you?" Randall finished.

Cold resolve entered the mate's eyes. "Aye, aye, Mr. Randall. What are your orders?"

"Get us out of here! We have to get the ship away from spying eyes and fast! I'll explain the rest once were under way."

"Aye, aye, matey! Consider us gone!"

Chapter Twenty-Two
The Coral Death

"Impossible!" A torrent of curses came from Nomar Samadi and his hooded boss. They could not understand the strange phenomena of the yacht leaving its moorings at the last moment before it was to be sunk.

"But what happened to LaPorte?" Samadi wanted to know, as he pushed past Captain Hazzard to look through the holes in the wall. "None of this makes any sense?"

Hazzard peered over the man's shoulder, through the coral window and saw the Cora Marie disappear in the mist of the morning. Again his quiet smile played about his lips. Randall had received his message of warning, dealt with the mysterious diver and was now moving the ship to safety. All was going according to plan.

"Look!" Samadi exclaimed, as he continued to look down into the water where the ship had been anchored. "There, in its wake, see... red froth... the water is red with blood! And shark fins everywhere!"

The hooded leader inched closer to his own portal and caught his breath behind his mask. Sure enough, the area Samadi had pointed out was a maelstrom of deadly activity and the mastermind of Lost Island knew the fate of the one called LaPorte. He backed away from the hole, grateful Hazzard couldn't see how truly shaken he was.

Seeing the smile on his prisoner only fueled his rising anger. "I wouldn't smile so soon, Captain Hazzard. "You won't escape so easily. I promise you that.

"You and the others may wish you were still within that steel ball at the bottom of the sea by the time I'm through with you." He motioned to Samadi and his Dyaks to bring them along. "Come, let me show a new death that will make fear surge through your veins. Samadi swears you do not know the meaning of the word. But I don't believe him, Captain. You have yet to witness the Coral Death!"

Captain Hazzard, Cole, Rima and Thomas Floyd were herded down another passageway off which small, room-like cells opened. As they turned one corner, Hazzard's keen eyesight picked out a small brown object discarded amongst empty boxes and other refuse stacked against the passage wall. He recognized the dead little monkey as Azlea O'Hara's beloved pet. The one and the same that had been instrumental in orchestrating their escape from the venomous cobras. Not wanted to distress the others, he kept silent and did not point it out. The poor creature didn't deserve its violent end, Hazzard added it to lists of wrongs he would avenge. A door was reached, and the man in the hood opened it, waved the four captives within. Captain Hazzard froze at the macabre tableau before them. Rima screamed, and swooned against Thomas Floyd who held her in his arms, his own eyes wide with shock.

It was a red room of horror, this cubicle of the Coral Death. On one side of the wall were three shallow tanks hollowed from blocks of red coral. The tanks were filled to the rim with water. Strange electrical devices hung over the water and the buzzing spit of high voltage could be heard.

And, moaning in delirium, three people were in the tanks of the Coral Death! Otto Van Dyke, Paul Dupres and Azlea O'Hara!

The horror of it tugged at Captain Hazzard's throat. For coral growths of red encrusted the three prisoners to the waist! The horrible red excrescence adhered tightly to the skin of the three in the tanks, was slowly but surely covering their bodies in a shell of crimson death!

In a few more days the red beastliness of the coral would sap their last living breaths, suffocate their bodies, then continue until they were encased in living rock.

"Poor, LaPorte," the hooded man sighed. "This was his crowning achievement! But how does this affect you, Captain Hazzard? Does fear now course through your blood, make shudders of dread race up your spine?"

Captain Hazzard laughed.

Nomar Samadi raised his gun and cocked it and touched the barrel to the back of Hazzard's head. "Please, master! Let me kill the fool now!"

"NO!" panted the hooded leader, "a bullet is too quick, too painless. But we must work fast, Samadi! These three now in the throes of the Coral Death will be covered in another twelve hours. We will finish them first."

The masked fiend turned to one of the bigger Dyaks. "Take them away and lock them up. Keep a guard on them at all times!"

As Hazzard and his people were marched out of the red room, the possessor of the Red Maggot gave Nomar Samadi further instructions. "We will have to work fast, double the charge of electrical energy, for in a few days that accursed yacht will return, perhaps with reinforcements. We want the island to be free of all our enemies when it inspected!"

Thomas Floyd and the still unconscious girl were ushered into an empty cell and then Hazzard and the cowboy were shoved into the next along the winding corridor. As the windowless door slammed shut behind them and the lock bolt slapped into place, they were instantly engulfed in darkness.

His hands out in front of his face, Jake Cole paced off eight feet before encountering the room's rock wall. He turned and whistled. "Well, we're in a pickle now. Ain't we, chief?"

In the dark, Captain Hazzard's voice was calm, exuding confidence. "Not to worry, Jake. Randall received my message and was able to save the ship.'

"Then you think he's going to get here in time to help us?"

"That is my hope. If he manages to locate their hidden harbor, then everything should fall into place. For now, I suggest you sit down on the floor and conserve your strength. When the time comes, things are going to get very hot around here."

Taking his own advice, Captain Hazzard folded his legs together and sat on the hard rock floor. He slowed his breathing and allowed his mind to relax, to be open and receptive. His last image of the *Cora Marie* sailing into the thick bothered him. If the mist did not

"Please, master! Let me kill the fool now!."

dissipate soon, finding the hooded man's anchorage might prove impossible for Tyler Randall.

If that were the case, then the final action against their captors would be left entirely to him and Cole, against some twenty armed Dyaks. Despite his natural optimism and faith in his cause, those were odds that even Captain Hazzard prayed to avoid.

****

Tyler Randall banked the SeaBee, swept over the sea toward Lost Island for a third time. Next to him in the co-pilot's seat, Hank Carter had all he could do to keep from turning green.

"Do you have to fly so blasted low to those rocks?" he inquired, his stomach rolling with each pass of the speedy amphibian.

"Keep your eyes out the window," Randall replied. "There has to be a way aboard this hunk rock that we aren't seeing."

"How do you know that for sure?"

"How else would Van Dyke and his people have set up a base of operation?"

"Yeah, and what about that? We've gone over the bloody island three times and there ain't one hut or tent anywhere in sight!"

Randall was frustrated that he could not tell the seamen the truth, that the cliffs were honeycombed with passages, natural caves that had been converted into Otto Van Dyke's pearl making operation on Lost Island. Since he had received this information via Captain Hazzard's telepathic messages, there was no way he could explain his knowledge without revealing the process involved, something Hazzard demanded remain confidential among his aides. The ability to communicate using telepathy was an advantage he was not about to nullify by sharing it with the rest of the world.

The more Randall imagined the secret complex beneath them, the more it made sense how Van Dyke had kept this insignificant coral landmass off the navigation charts and thus been able to protect his investment for so long.

"Senor, look down there!" Manuel Ramirez suddenly called out from his seat in the rear of the cabin. "To port, where the big rocks rise out of the sea."

Holding the controls tightly, Randall raised the nose of the aircraft and brought her around again, this time dropping even lower over the sharp cliffs that jutted out of the Java Sea to a height of a hundred feet.

"There!" the little Mexican cried. "See the big black spot?"

As the SeaBee dropped nose first towards the pounding waves, Randall saw a huge area of the cliff face which seemed covered but a huge shadow, until he realized the sun was hitting the wall directly.

"GEEZ! PULL UP!" Carter begged!

Randall was happy to comply, as he had seen enough to know they had found their target. As the powerful seaplane lifted its nose and flew over several giant boulders, Randall knew they had found a natural grotto that cut into the heart of the island. Now it was time to set down and investigate. As he prepared to land on the choppy water, he silently sent out his mental news to Captain Hazzard.

We've found it! We're on our way, Captain!

Chapter Twenty-Three
A Villian Unmasked

An hour had passed since Captain Hazzard and Jake Cole were locked up in the small, square room. Suddenly Hazzard reached out and caught Cole's arm, held it tightly for long seconds. Then, the small flashlight from one of his many pouches flared on and Cole saw his boss smiling broadly.

"Are you ready?" he asked softly.

Jake Cole nodded eagerly as Hazzard handed him the tiny torch. Cole watched as his employer bent over and wrenched the heel from his right boot, then the left. Inside the hollow spaces disclosed were two "palm" pistols, a dozen small bullets. Captain Hazzard divided the bullets, handed the cowboy one of the tiny guns. From another of his belt pockets, he took a small steel box which, when opened, yielded a handful of marble-sized glass balls.

Then he walked to the door, inspected the iron hinges. Careful not to break the glass balls before he was ready, he placed one on top of each hinge, resting it against the door itself. Then he tapped them with the small palm gun. The glass shattered and smoking acid ran down the iron hinge. It corroded the iron immediately, began to eat into the metal structure, dissolve it as hot water melts ice.

Then, after making his intentions known to Cole, they lunged against the door simultaneously. It fell to the floor of the outer passage, crushing the hapless Dyak who had been standing guard. As Hazzard leaped over the fallen door, the second guard across the hall, threw his kris knife. Luckily his aim was off and the razor sharp blade thunked against the wall over Hazzard's right shoulder. He started to fire his palm pistol, decided against making any further noise. Instead he rushed the still dazed native and felled him with a strong right cross to the chin.

Hurriedly Captain Hazzard yanked the bolt from the other door and pulled it open. Thomas Floyd stumbled out, followed by a dazed and frightened Rima Van Dyke. They both brightened at the sight of Hazzard and Jake Cole. Hazzard held a finger to his lips to caution them.

"Floyd," he whispered. "Can you and Rima find the red room from here?"

"Yes, I'm pretty sure I can retrace the way there," the Skipper nodded.

"Good, take this then," Captain Hazzard handed Floyd his palm pilot. "But don't use it unless you have no other choice. Now you and Rima find that torture chamber and free her father and the others."

"You can count on me, Captain."

"I know, old man. Once you've freed those poor souls, barricade yourselves in that room and don't come out until you hear from me or Jake. Is that understood?"

"Perfectly." Thomas Floyd shook Hazzard's hand strongly. "Good luck to you two. Give those rats a few knocks for me while you're at it!"

As Floyd turned to proceed on their assigned mission, Rima stood on her toes and planted a fast kiss on Hazzard's cheek. He smiled and watched them hurry away down the dimly lit corridor. Jake came to his side and winked.

"Here you go, boss," he handed Hazzard a kris knife. "You might need this."

"Thanks, Jake," Captain Hazzard breathed softly in the cowboy's ear. "Now to the central room!"

Their weapons in hand, the two stole silently down the winding passageway to the main room sixty yards away. Coming around a curve in the hall, they saw it ahead of them, saw too a portion of a man's back seated at the desk.

Unobserved, they reached the room. It was Nomar Samadi seated at the desk. Captain Hazzard, his jaw grim, his blue-gray eyes hard, stepped into view, strode silently across until he stood at Samadi's back.

"Get up, Samadi, I've come for you!" Hazzard rapped out.

Nomar Samadi leaped to his feet knocking over his chair, face pale and lips curled away from his white teeth. He was panting with sudden fear, and his eyes stared wide. But rats fight when they are cornered. His arrowing form flashed at Hazzard. Together, locked in each others arms, they sprawled to the floor.

The murderer fought like a tiger with kicking feet, nails, his teeth. Captain Hazzard hammered in a flashing fist which caught Samadi on the cheek. He went back and down. Hazzard was on him like a pouncing puma. Once more fist flashed, and this time it found the target of Samadi's jaw. His body went lax. Hazzard rose to his feet.

"Stand where you are, Captain Hazzard!"

Across the room, gun in hand, stood the man in the hood! Captain Hazzard, eyes wintry, dove to his right as the villain fired. The shot went wide and the criminal overlord brought his pistol around for a second try.

Suddenly from the rear entrance another pistol cracked and the masked villain was struck in the arm.

Jake Cole, still in the doorway, frantically began reloading the single-shot palm gun. Maddened by his wound, his left arm bleeding and numb at his side, the villain took aim on the cowboy. This time he would not miss!

On his knees, Captain Hazzard pulled the kris knife from his belt and flung it with deadly accuracy. The blade struck the killer in the chest, directly into his heart. His gun fired towards the roof and he gave a terrible cry that split the confines of the room, echoed and re-echoed through the grisly red passages. The man in the hood clasped the knife buried in his chest, fell forward on his face...

"Where's Samadi?" Cole yelled.

Hazzard turned. Samadi's body had disappeared! During the fight with the hooded leader Samadi had regained consciousness, crawled away. Suddenly screams of fury filled the room and a score of dacoits and Malays boiled at Captain Hazzard and the cowboy. Jake managed to get off a final shot from his palm gun, dropping the nearest Dyak, then the useless weapon was knocked from his hand.

Captain Hazzard managed to dig out several Whistling Devils and flung them into the oncoming rush of brown bodies. As the screeching whistles started up and the blanket of gray, noxious gas jetted forth, the confused natives were halted in their tracks. Soon their eyes were smarting and their lungs burning. It was all the opportunity Hazzard needed to wade into them, fists flying and legs kicking. Grunts and moans arose from the melee of battling figures lost in the thick cloud of smoke now filling the room.

Meanwhile Jake Cole had also managed to drop several of his attackers, but their numbers were too great and he was backed into a corner from which there was no escape. Gritting his teeth and wishing he had a stick of gum, the lanky Montana wrangler kept flailing away with his punches, even as returning blows began to take their toll.

Giving with a loud roar, Captain Hazzard, his tunic torn to shreds, emerged from the thick chemical haze, hurling smaller men off him like a bear dispatching a pack of wolves. But the natives were obsessed with the fever of the Red Maggot, and kris in hands, fell on him ruthlessly, determined to bring him down no matter the cost to their own number.

A fierce yell that sounded like a banshee wail of death split the ears of the yowling natives. The next moment Tyler Randall, Hank Carter and Manuel Ramirez, guns blazing, were in the thick of the fray! Their guns bucked under their stead grips, threw death at the surprised natives.

It was all the diversion Captain Hazzard and Jake Cole needed to recover and throw off their attackers. Within seconds each of them had accounted for another six dacoits knocked senseless. And then it was over. The island was conquered! And in the thick of the brown bodies lay the dead Nomar Samadi, finally brought down by a bullet to the head.

After the remaining natives had surrendered and herded away empty cells by First Mate Carter with help from the porky Mexican cook, Captain Hazzard, Jake Cole and Tyler Randall stood over the lifeless figure of the Hooded Man.

"I wanna to see that owl hoot's face!" Cole growled as he bent over the dead man.

Captain Hazzard laughed. "I can tell you who it is, Jake. It's – Jubal Beck! I caught him several times rubbing his chin with a forefinger, and I remembered Beck's habit. Then when he saw the Cora

Marie sailing off, he got so excited, he spoke in his own voice and I recognized it immediately."

"But why, Captain?" Tyler asked as the cowboy peeled off the brown hood to bare the face of Jubal Beck. "After working for Mr. Van Dyke for so long, how did he come to this?"

"I can only believe it was the Red Maggot, Randall. He probably has it on his person somewhere.

"My guess is over the years he became warped with the desire to own it and from that madness evolved the rest of his wild scheme. He was behind it all. That phony attack on him in New York was to divert suspicion. On one of his trips to the Far East he must have made the contacts and plans for the capture of the Red Maggot."

Ten minutes later Thomas Floyd, Rima Van Dyke and the freed prisoners of Lost Island were together again celebrating their narrow escape from death. The three who had suffered at the hands of Jubal Beck and Nomar Samadi were weak and tired, but hey would recover given time. Rima Van Dyke was in the arms of her father and Paul Dupres. Azlea, abashed and confused, stood in the background, trembling. Jake Cole found a blanket and gently wrapped the girl up, allowing her to lean back on him.

Azlea looked up into his friendly smile and blurted out, "Samadi killed my little pet. He broke its neck in front of me!" Then she became to sob and buried her head on his chest.

Seeing all this, Rima turned to Captain Hazzard. "Azlea has suffered enough, Captain. If it is alright with you, I'd like her to stay her on the island with Paul and me."

"That's very generous of you, Rima," Hazzard saw Azlea looking towards him and he smiled warmly. "The poor girl can use a good friend like you. Thank you."

As the girl moved off, Captain Hazzard turned to Tyler Randall. "Well, I take it you found their hidden harbor."

"Yes, sir! It was just as you figured out, Captain. It's on the other side of the island from the pearl beds. It's a huge grotto that cuts into the cliff. Mr. Van Dyke's people built a pier inside and we found the Chinese dhow we'd been trapped on back in Singapore that night.

"There was also another seaplane moored there as well." Added the tall, blonde pilot, happy he and two crewmen had arrived in time.

"It must have belonged to Beck."

"Yes, it's how he got here so fast," Captain Hazzard agreed. "Which wraps up all the loose ends, Randall. Our friends have been rescued and Jubal Beck's evil plans to disrupt the pearl markets and cause nation revolts among the island governments is thwarted." A strange look came over the champion of justice and he spoke another line as if to himself. "At least for the time being."

Otto Van Dyke, breaking away from the others, approached and extended his hand to Hazzard. As they shook, his weary, unshaven face was almost to the point of tears. "There is nothing I can say, Captain Hazzard, except, thank you."

"Nothing else need be said, sir," Hazzard offered humbly.

"Ah, yes, I know. You were merely pursuing your life's duty. You are a remarkable, man, Captain." Otto Van Dyke was serious for a moment. "But there is one thing I want to do while we are all here. I want the memory of a gallant gentlemen to remain with you – with us – always. And," his smile was tremulous, "you are always welcome to return to – Wells Island!

"I hereby dedicate it, erase for all time the fear of a superstitious force causing the natives to wish to drive us away."

"Then I reckon you'll be needin' this doohickey," Jake Cole held out his hand and in it was the blood red pearl, the Red Maggot.

The old German nodded, took the heart-shaped pearl in his hands, held it up for all to see, then dropped it onto the coral floor, ground it to dust under his heel! "For you, Jonathan, my old friend," and his voice cracked.

Captain Hazzard, the picture of Jonathan Wells large in his memory, brought his hand up in a stiff salute.

Epilogue

"What a great story!" William Crawley editorialized as he finished scribbling in his pocket-sized notebook. The thing was nearly filled with his rushed script, all hastily jotted down while listening to Captain Hazzard's account of the Red Maggot.

It was over a month since Hazzard, Jake Cole and Tyler Randall had returned from their South Seas jaunt with Thomas Floyd aboard his ship, the Cora Marie. Since that time, all of them had once again settled into the routines of Hazzard Labs. Still, other in-city assignments, over the past couple of weeks, had kept Crawley from coming over and getting the scoop.

As always, his pal, pulp writer Chester Hawks was anxious to get another of Captain Hazzard's true life exploits down on paper for all his thousands of fans world-wide.

Now, sitting here in the main lounge of the Captain's private quarters, Crawley was also enjoying the company of his associates, Washington MacGowen and Martin Tracey. Tracey's dark brown hair was almost an inch long now, after having been shaved bald in their last adventure by doctors working for Circe Yu Sun. As Hazzard had regaled them with his exciting tale, Tracey had poured them each a generous portion of brandy. All save Captain Hazzard who never drank alcohol of any kind. He enjoyed sipping a tall glass of orange juice.

Outside a cold winter storm had settled in and just as Crawley had driven through the front gates of the complex, a powdery snowfall had begun.

"Well, I'm glad you enjoyed it," Hazzard finished. "And I'm also very glad we all lived to pass it along."

"I sure wish I could have gone along," Martin Tracey sighed, taking a small sip of his brandy. "The warm South Seas, exotic native girls, tropical isles. It all sounds like paradise to me."

"Ha," Hazzard laughed at his first cousin. "Had you seen the sea-snakes, the sharks and crocodiles, I'm not so sure you would be calling it paradise. There were lots of elements of that other less heavenly place as well."

"Well, whatever it was," Crawley almost crowed with delight. "You've given me a rip-roaring story. Your fans are going to eat this up."

"There is one more thing I would ask you to do while discussing your notes with Hawks, Bill."

"Sure, Captain. What is it?"

"The current political situation in that part of the world is fragile and not at all healthy for the future of mankind."

"I don't understand. How do you mean?"

"Colonialism, Bill. It's an archaic, evil expansion tool that too many western countries have used to cruelly subjugate and exploit the natives of the South Seas. Its practices must end before the unrest and suffering they have created foment into bloody revolutions."

"Wow, Captain, I didn't realize you were so passionate about the subject."

"He's more than that," Wash MacGowen joined in. "He's going to Washington next week to talk with the Secretary of State on just that topic. I'll be tagging along, as I've a few good contacts in the Capital. Together we should get our case heard."

"Good for you," Crawley applauded and began writing more notes in his small journal. "Keep me posted on how that all goes, will you?"

Captain Hazzard stood up from his padded leather chair and nodded. "Of course, Bill. But right now, it's time to add another piece to our collection of mementos." He walked over to the three glass cases lining the back wall of the expansive, richly decorated study. One held a garish feathered head mask crafted from a giant South American anaconda. Next to it, in the second case, resting snuggly on the featureless form of a plastic mannequin's head was metallic silver band covered with electrical wires. Martin Tracey shivered at the sight of it and unconsciously reached out to touch his own temple. This was the very mind-control band that had turned him into a slave of the Green Dragon.

Hazzard stopped by the third and final case and was joined there by his mentor, Professor MacGowen. The case was empty but for a small velvet case that lay open inside it.

"So what's going in there?" Crawley asked getting to his feet.

"This," Captain Hazzard answered and held the bright red, uncut ruby given to him by the Dyak chief, M'La.

"Holy smokes," the crime reporter exclaimed, "that thing is as big as a chocolate Easter egg!?"

"It's the gift from a new friend," Hazzard said as MacGowen lifted up the glass bubble and allowed him to place the precious gem in the middle of the velvet box. The light from the overhead lamps caused it to sparkle as if aflame. All of them were momentarily mesmerized by its brilliance.

Just then the front door swung open and Jake Cole came walking in, a mischievous look on his face. "Hey, chief, we got us some company."

Cole stepped off to the side and Otto Van Dyke, wearing a heavy top coat, muffler and bowler hat appeared behind him. There were flecks of snow on his shoulders. He spotted Hazzard and smiled.

"Ah, Captain, please forgive this unannounced visit at such a late hour, but she simply refused to listen to reason."

"She?"

Another, smaller figure, emerged behind the two men and Captain Hazzard's eyes blinked. Azlea O'Hara, dressed to the nines in the most stylish, western clothes, complete with soft leather boots and matching gloves, came running across the room, arms spread wide.

"Captain Hazzard! It is me, Azlea! I have traveled all around the world to be here with you!"

Hazzard's three companions were all agog, their looks going back and forth like witnessing a tennis match, as the beautiful young Eurasian woman closed the gap between herself and their stunned leader.

"You have?"

Azlea threw herself into his arms, and before Hazzard could stop

*"It is me, Azlea! I have traveled around
the world to be here with you!"*

her, she pulled his neck down and planted a long, tender kiss on his lips. MacGowen, Crawley and Tracey were aghast and doing their best not to start laughing. It was near impossible.

"Geez, Captain," smirked Crawley. "Are you sure you told us everything that went on out there in the islands?"

Forcefully, Hazzard took the girl's arms and removed them from her neck, albeit still with care. "Please, Azlea," he politely begged. "Start from the beginning. I thought you were going to stay on Wells Island with Rima and her new husband, Paul Dupres?"

"Oh, but I was, Captain," the innocent lovely explained. "Then when I saw how sad Mr. Van Dyke was at leaving his only daughter behind to return to your country, I realized I should go with him."

"Excuse me?" Hazzard looked to the old jeweler for assistance. "What is she saying?"

"Well, it did make perfect sense," Otto Van Dyke said, holding his bowler in his hands. "Although I did protest at first, the idea of living in that big apartment downtown all by myself was certainly not appealing. Besides, as one of the regents at Eastgate College, I could easily transfer my daughter's paid tuition to Azlea so she could benefit from a good, college education. She'll live there most of the time and spend her holidays with me. It will be like having another daughter."

"Isn't that wonderful, Captain?" Azlea couldn't contain her exuberance. "I am going to go to college and become a real, all-American girl. That way, you and I can be together some day."

"What?"

"Oh, I know you have devoted your life to battling injustice, and evil but I will fight along side you, Captain. And some day, when the battle is over, and you choose to live as other men, then I will be here for you, my darling.

"As Mrs. Captain Hazzard!"

Jake Cole started laughing and soon everyone else, including Otto Van Dyke had joined in.

Azlea turned and looked at them with confusion. "Did I say something funny?"

Kevin Douglas Hazzard shook his head and laughter filled his heart.

The End

Afterward

WELCOME TO THE NEW AIRSHIP 27

Welcome to the new **Airship 27 Productions** and this re-edited edition of our third Captain Hazzard adventure, **Curse Of The Red Maggot.**

Late in the winter of 2007, Rob Davis and I had the truly good fortune of meeting publisher Michael Poll of **Cornerstone Book Publishers.** Michael was looking to expand his publishing line and we were looking for a reliable publisher who could support our varied pulp projects.

It was one of those meetings made in heaven, you might say.

Once we realized the potential inherent in our joining forces, we quickly agreed on a partnership and began the process. Our two first books, **Witchfire** and **Brother Bones** soon hit the market place and have been selling extremely well. Thank you for your continued support of our efforts.

In reprinting these early volumes, Rob and I saw an opportunity to enhance them during the re-editing process. Some will have new features and others new covers or interior illustrations. Still our goal remains the same, to give you, our readers, the finest new pulp adventures possible. What follows is the edited post-text I wrote for this book when it was published. Enjoy.

THE LOST HAZZARD

If there is anything I love as much as pulps, its pulp fans. They come from all corners of society and parts of the world. Their common denominator, a true love of action-adventure fiction done pulp style. The more purple the prose, the better. You are now holding in your hands a book that would not have existed if it had not been for the enthusiasm of one of those fans. His name is Don O'Malley and he deserves the credit for not only this book but also for correcting an historical alteration that should never have occurred in the first place. Allow me to explain.

The first and only issue of Captain Hazzard appeared in 1938. It had been produced by A.A. Wyn's Magazine Publishers Incorporated to be another Doc Savage and that first adventure, **Python Men Of The Lost City,** was churned out by their top writer, Paul Chadwick. Chadwick was best known for his work on the company's only successful hero tile, Secret Agent X. For whatever reasons, lack of sales, reader response or editorial disinterest, there never was a second issue.

But there was, really. You see, it was generally believed by pulp historians that Chadwick had in fact written a second Hazzard adventure. Were the title to be successful as a monthly, it is only common sense to believe that as **Python Men** was going off to the presses they would have had a second script ready to go. But when the title folded so abruptly the editors found themselves holding a literary white elephant. Most likely having paid Chadwick for the second book, his editors would not have been content to merely let it sit on their shelves and collect dust.

Ultimately the script was taken and heavily rewritten/edited and turned into a Secret Agent X story entitled **The Curse of the Crimson Horde.** Upon reading this story one quickly encounters so many oddities as to quickly comprehend this is no ordinary Secret Agent X tale. It reads like something much more suited to a globe trotting adventure rather than disguised super-spy.

When we began our launch of Captain Hazzard adventures with our new version of **Python Men Of The Lost City,** none of us knew how it would be received by the pulp community. Our fingers were tightly crossed. Happily our concerns were quickly laid to rest as the overwhelming feedback we began receiving from our readers was very positive. Many of you who picked up that book even went as far as to hunt up a reprint of the original and compared the two versions to see what changes I had wrought. I was thrilled and set about getting ready to the first all new Captain Hazzard book, **Citadel Of Fear,** with my colleague, Martin Powell.

A few months later, as we were plotting **Citadel Of Fear,** I received a very interesting e-mail from pulp fan, Don O'Malley. Having picked up **Python Men Of The Lost City** and enjoyed it, Don wanted to know if I had intentions of ever seeking out that peculiar Secret Agent X story, **The Curse Of The Crimson Horde,** and turning it back into a Captain Hazzard adventure. To be honest, the thought had never entered my mind. I replied to Don that it was a very intriguing idea but I had no idea where I could find that book, should I ever decide to go down that road. Of course Don wasn't about to let me off the hook that easily. He immediately came back to that he owned that very story and would gladly make me a Xerox copy of for my files. I was pleasantly taken aback by his generosity and told him to go ahead and send it to me. Several weeks later a huge package arrived by mail and in it was the entire issue of Secret Agent X magazine containing the story, **The Curse Of The Crimson Horde.** I was mildly amused and put it on a shelf in my office. Maybe some day I'd get around to it and see what could be done.

Of course, if you are holding this book, you realize "someday" came a lot sooner than I had expected. Martin Powell and I writing **Citadel Of Fear** in tandem, each of us doing a few chapters and then sending off the script to the other. Somewhere in the middle of the project, Powell's day job forced him to do some traveling and he wrote me saying he would have to hold off on his chapters for a few weeks. There was nothing else to be done. As the days rolled by, I began to get restless and kept thinking of that package O'Malley had sent me. Hmm, alright, I thought, let's take a look at it.

After reading only a few pages, I was hooked. The theory put forth by pulp historians was so obviously correct right from the start. This had clearly been intended to be a Captain Hazzard novel! And so I bit the bullet and began rewriting **The Curse Of The Crimson Horde** pretty much the same way I had done with **Python Men,** only now the challenge would be a lot harder. Now I would have to interpret Paul Chadwick's scenes and try to re-imagine them as he had originally put them down on paper in 1938. The thing was, and I did not realize it immediately, my earlier experience of rewriting Chadwick had made his style familiar to me. Thus as I set about changing his sea-going adventure, I found myself second guessing where the plot was going pages ahead of what I was working on. It was spooky to say the least. It was as if I was looking over his shoulder, seeing those original pages and going back to them, all the while adding my own personal touches.

So here it is, finished. What started out as Captain Hazzard # 2 and then became a Secret Agent X episode is now our Captain Hazzard # 3. And since we were going to be returning the tale to its true beginnings, I thought to change both the title and the by-line.

The blood red pearl that is the focus of the entire plot is called the Red Maggot. Somehow that struck me as being much more pulpish than Crimson Horde. Secondly Paul Chadwick certainly would have used many different pseudonyms in his career as a pulpsmith. He wrote his Secret Agent X books as Brant House and created that one and only Captain Hazzard as Chester Hawks. Now had this story appeared on the newsstands in 1938 as a Hazzard book, that is the name that would have glared at you on the news racks. So it was only fitting that **The Curse Of The Red Maggot** be credited to yours truly and the amazingly talented, hard working, Chester Hawks.

There you have it, the story behind the story. A big tip of the pulp fedora to Mr. Don O'Malley for lighting a fire under me to get this done. But please, Don, don't go finding me any more "lost"

Hazzards. Ha. From now on, I'm going to be concentrating on his "all new" adventures. And believe me there are lots more of those on the way starting with **Cavemen Of New York** which I've just completed and we now have in pre-production.

We hope to have it published within a month or so of this release.

As always, we here at Airship 27 welcome your comments and ideas. My e-mail is listed below. Feel free to drop me a line. Till then, take care and keep reading pulps.

They're good for you.

Ron Fortier

28 Jan. 2008
Somersworth, N.H.
(www.Airship27.com)
(Airship27@comcast.net)

Airship **27**

An interview with
Rob Davis

AIRSHIP-27 So tell us, Rob, did you always know you wanted to be an artist? Did this knowledge come to you as a child or later in life?

Rob Davis: It was around eight when I first had the idea I could draw. It was around this same time comics entered my life via a friend and the deal was sealed. I can even tell you what comic book did the deed-- it was Jack Kirby's Marvel Comics work on Avengers #2. Something about how those pages just seemed alive that did it.

AIR-27: What were some of your earliest influences? Which artists and illustrators inspired your own career?

Davis: As I mentioned Jack Kirby's work at Marvel Comics in the 60's was very inspirational. The characters and situations just seemed to leap off the page at you. I was hooked. There are loads of others from Steve Ditko to Curt Swan and Gil Kane-- and these are the ones that are obvious, there are others I'm not even aware influenced me and others point out to me.

AIR-27: So how about a informal biography of your career as an artist? Where there projects that stand out in your mind as exceptional

Captain
Kevin Douglas
Hazzard

*Adventurer, scientist, explorer,
and Champion of Justice.*

Dr. Martin Tracey

Skilled surgeon, boxer, and playboy

and others you'd rather forget? And why so for both?

Davis: I almost hate to highlight my early work. I look at it now and ask myself how it ever got past the editors! (HA!)

My first professional work was as an illustrator of role playing games. I did module spot illustrations for Mayfair Games' DC Heroes game as well as Iron Crown's Champions super hero role playing game. I parlayed that into lettering and inking work at NOW comics, eventually being allowed to pencil. After severing my connections with NOW I got hooked up with what became Malibu Comics, starting out with a rather racy character named *Scimidar* with writer R.A. Jones. R.A. and I also did a couple of mini-series based on the character Merlin while there.

From there I tried to use my interest in realistic portraiture to get work on what was my absolute favorite project, Star Trek. Starting with Quantum Leap at Innovation (where I also did another project: Straw Men, as well as an issue of Maze Agency) I worked that into a one-shot at DC on Star Trek and then jumped back to Malibu when they got the rights to do *Deep Space Nine*, staying with them until the licenses, and Malibu, were bought up by Marvel Comics. After that I kicked around a bit from Arrow Comics, to Caliber (notably on a series called *Robyn of Sherwood* that the creator/writer Paul Storrie and I are "re-mastering" for a reintroduction sometime in the next year or so), but by then the independent companies I'd been working with were dying off and the Star Trek licenses at Marvel, and then Wildstorm, were faltering. So I "semi-retired" from comics after that, though with the resurgence in the industry I'm finding a bit more to do these days.

Let me mention that early in this story Ron Fortier contacted me to do some work on NOW comics' Green Hornet series, which after all these years has resulted in my working with him on these pulp character revival books. So it's funny how it comes full circle.

AIR-27: What is the one character you've drawn that gave you the most satisfaction? Is there a particular fictional character you'd love to get your creative teeth into? And why that character?

Davis: The first question is a tough one. My first real success came with *Scimidar* with R.A. Jones at Malibu, so I'd say I had a great deal of satisfaction working on that character and with R.A. There was a level of synergy on the book that I've only come close to a couple of times. Most recently the work I did with Ron Fortier on DAUGHTER OF DRACULA was another of those times when what we each brought to the final product emphasized what the other did. A kind of "more than the sum of its parts" kind of thing. That always seems to happen with female characters with me.

As for your second question, I have a couple and they're closely related, literally! I have never done a western comic or illustrated a western story. I'd LOVE to do something with The Lone Ranger or something similar in a comics setting. And I have regretted turning Ron down on drawing the Green Hornet so many years ago, and as most pulp fans know, the Hornet is the Lone Ranger's great nephew. I'd settle for doing spot illustrations in a pulp-like novel, but doing a full blown comic on either or both of these guys would be a great thrill for me. I can't say much about it right now, but the wish to do a western character may yet be fulfilled on a project that I'm not at liberty to discuss yet...

AIR-27: Writer Ron Fortier is the other half of Airship 27 Productions and perhaps your biggest fan. How did the two of you first hook up?

Davis: As I noted earlier, Ron contacted me to draw the Green Hornet at NOW comics. At the time my relations with NOW were strained and I just couldn't do the project, though I really was thrilled at the prospect of drawing the Hornet. Ron understood, and pitched me another idea that we did a proposal for at DC: Rose and Thorn. That didn't work out either, unfortunately. It was a wonderful story and could really have done well I think. After that Ron and I exchanged Christmas Cards off and on until years later when he ran into my "The Spirit of Rt. 66" web comic.

AIR-27: How do you like your new career as a pulp illustrator?

Prof. Washington "Wash" MacGowen

Genius physicist,
mathematician,
and electrical wizard

Tyler Randall

*Test pilot, engineering inventor,
and mechanic*

Pulps were all but a forgotten genre until outfits like Airship 27 began producing all new books. Do you think there is a place for pulps in today's market?

Davis: This has been, and is, a blast to do. The Pulps are the precursor to comic books. Characters like Superman, Batman, etc. can trace their roots directly to the pulps and the Shadow, the Spider, Doc Savage and so on. So it's only natural that my interest in comics leads back down the trail to the pulp characters that inspired them. I'm really exercising the same art "muscle" here, using different workout machinery!

As for today's pulp market if you just look around at all media these days pulp influences are everywhere! James Bond, Batman, The X-Men movies, TV's Heroes, Lost-- the list is long. Given this I think pulp already has the market, it's just a matter of letting people know where the roots of all this came from.

AIR-27: The first pulp project you worked on to feature classic characters was THE HOUNDS OF HELL, which featured Doctor Satan and the Moon Man in the first ever pulp cross-over. How did you enjoy working on classic characters like these two pulp icons?

Davis: Well, my first work with Ron was on a web comic about Dr. Satan for the now defunct Adventurestrips.com. Like the first Captain Hazzard book, it was a re-tooling of an original pulp tale, the first appearance of Dr. Satan and his nemesis, Ascott Keane. A wild but fun ride down pulp lane. So it was natural that he asked me to illustrate the crossover since it was a continuation of that working relationship. As far as my feelings about it, as I mentioned before, the pulp characters are the ancestors of the comic book characters I grew up with in the 60's and that inspired me to draw. I've always loved characters like Tarzan, the Lone Ranger, The Green Hornet, etc., and all those were pulp characters, though when I first met them they were in another medium, film or TV. It's a great thrill to be able to breathe some new life into some of the lesser known pulp characters as well as Ron's newest creation, Brother Bones.

AIR-27: You did a Doctor Satan comic strip prior to this book. Tell us a little something about that project, please.

Davis: Well, Dr. Satan was a pulp villain steeped in the occult who disguised himself in a garish red outfit with a cowl adorned with horns. His opponent was Ascott Keane, kind of a cross between Sherlock Holmes and The Avenger or any of a number of other pulp heroes who used disguises regularly. Ron Fortier was inspired to re-tell the first Dr. Satan tale in comics format for the fledgling web comics format and asked me if I'd draw it for him, keeping to a weekly deadline. I'm happy to brag that from start to finish we kept true to that deal, though there were some close calls. This was not an easy task given that I have a family and full-time job. The full comic is archived on my website.

AIR-27: The obvious flagship series of the new Airship 27 Productions is the Captain Hazzard series. What kind of experience has this been for you brining to life the Champion of Justice and his Fighting Five?

Davis: Actually, my work is based on earlier incarnations from artists who had done some preliminary work on Captain Hazzard before me. Ron had some definite ideas about how he wanted Cap and his team members to look, and he told me which aspects of each of those earlier renderings he liked best. I just put those together as smoothly as I could to Ron's specifications. He's had some very specific critiques and corrections made along the way too when I stray from his vision. Now, some artists might find that bothersome, but my motto in doing what I do artistically is to do "what best serves the story." These have been Ron's (and in the second book additionally Martin Powell's) story so what Ron asks for I do my best to deliver. Despite this, I've had plenty of leeway in how I depict most things. In addition, I've had plenty of research to do trying to get the period costumes, machines, and settings to fit the time in which these stories are told, the 1930's in the USA. Much as

William "Bill" Crawley

Ace crime reporter for a metropolitan newspaper.

Jake Cole

*Sharpshooter, expert tracker,
and lariat master*

I did when I worked on the Star Trek comic books, I enjoy trying to get things "right" for the period and setting.

AIR-27: As of this writing you've illustrated four Captain Hazzard books. Can you tell us which of these characters is your favorite and why he (or she) is so special to you?

Davis: Wow, great question and a tough one. The females I've drawn so far are always a favorite subject for this red-blooded American Male artist, as I am a great admirer of the beauty of the female form, but the character that seems the most fun to do that's on a regular basis has to be Jake Cole. The ten-gallon hat, the six-shooter, the whole down-home attitude. Visually he's the most interesting (besides the women, of course!), though our hero, Captain Hazzard certainly has a great visual look as well.

AIR-27: When doing the illustrations for one of these books, who determines which scenes will be chosen, you or the writer? And do you always agree on the choices made?

Davis: I've been given pretty much full reign on what scenes to draw. What I usually do is count the number of chapters and divide that by the number of illustrations (usually nine) and then try to space the illustrations out evenly through the book. Occasionally though a particular scene will scream out for depiction and I've even had to add an extra illustration to the book because of it. I have yet to have any complaints or objections to my choices, though I've often surprised the writer with what I pick. I don't always pick the most action filled scene. Sometimes I pick the emotional heart of the chapter, and that's not always an action scene.

AIR-27: Besides interior work, you've also done several pulp covers, front and back. Is it difficult to come up with new designs and ideas all the time? Do you ever get an artist version of a writer's block? And if you, what do you do to break through it?

Davis: Being on deadline as a comics artist you just can't suffer

"Artists's Block" If you want to stay employed for very long. So what I learned to do when I hit the wall was just to sit at the table and just start moving the pencil around, even just doodling. Eventually that would get things flowing and the "Block" would melt away.

As far as running out of design ideas and characters- I must admit that I have a stable of "stock" characters in my repertoire, as do many cartoonists and illustrators. If I need something outside of that stock company I hit my "Morgue File" of magazine clippings that I keep in a file cabinet in the studio. Also, I love people watching at the Mall and at work. Many of my designs are based on observations I've made of real people who I've just exaggerated or made a few adjustments to. Plus, when I'm reading a story there's a film that plays in my head. I see the scenes as they play out. I may have to research how to do details on cars or boats or such, but generally the design of the scene has played out in my head first and I just pick the most interesting "frame" to illustrate.

AIR-27: Rob, we've taken up enough of your valuable time. Before leaving, are there any up and coming projects you would like to mention to our readers to include pulps and comics?

Davis: There are the numerous projects with Cornerstone as another Captain Hazzard novel (The Cave Men of New York) , a mini-series western I mentioned earlier with Ron Fortier that's making the rounds of the comics publishers right now, and an updating of a project I did with writer Paul Storrie back in the 90's called "Robyn of Sherwood" is being "remastered", as Paul likes to say, from the mini-series set in medieval Sherwood Forest into a completely re-drawn graphic novel. And I've been doing a weekly web editorial cartoon with old friend Jack Curtin since before George W. Bush was elected which is presently called thedubyachronicles.com. So I'm pretty busy!

AIR-27: Do you have a website where fans can visit and keep up with your many projects?

Davis: If any fans want to keep up with what's happening in my

Azlea O'Hara

*Linguist, martial arts student
and all around trouble-maker.*

studio they're welcome to drop by my website at: http://robmdavis. com/gallery.

AIR-27: Thanks so much for doing this, and best of luck with all your future endeavors.

Davis: Thanks for the interview. It's been a pleasure!

COMING SOON *IN THE NEXT THRILLING* INSTALLMENT OF CAPTAIN HAZZARD...

An evil genius of science has learned how to transform people into throwback savages bent on total destruction and has unleashed them throughout Manhattan.

In the midst of the greatest blizzard ever to hit the gotham, CAPTAIN HAZZARD and his Fighting Five must confront and battle...

The CAVEMEN of NEW YORK!!!

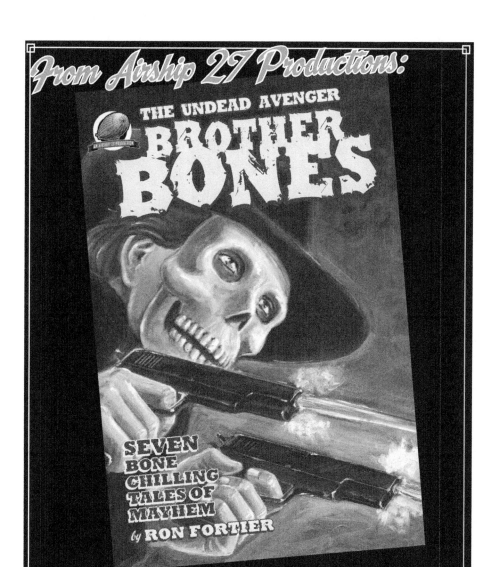